BRITISH AMERICAN
PUBLISHING

A Perfect Family

A Perfect Family

Darrell Husted

British American Publishing

This novel is a work of fiction. Names, characters, places and incidents either are the product of the author's imagination or are used fictitiously. Any resemblance to actual events or locales or persons, living or dead, is entirely coincidental.

Published by British American Publishing
3 Cornell Road
Latham, NY 12110
Manufactured in the United States of America

93 92 91 90 89 5 4 3 2 1

Library of Congress Cataloging in Publication Data

Husted, Darrell.
  A perfect family / Darrell Husted
    p. cm.
  ISBN 0–945167–02–4 : $17.95
  I. Title
PS3558.U7795P47 1988
813'.54—dc19   88–18819
                                                       CIP

A Perfect Family

Chapter One

ON THANKSGIVING MORNING, two days before all save one were murdered, Bill Johnson lined his family up in front of the kitchen drainboard to be photographed with the holiday turkey.

His eyes, behind black plastic frame glasses, were puffy from sleep, but he was happy. He stopped in front of the turkey and said, "By golly, I'm gonna take a picture of that."

Harriet, his wife, glanced at the bird—glaucous, and pimply from plucked feathers—and said absent-mindedly, "Maybe you ought to wait till it's cooked, hon." She turned from the drainboard where the turkey had thawed overnight; a pinkish rivulet of water-diluted blood had soaked through the white butcher's paper and dribbled into the sink. "What's everyone want for breakfast?" she asked, then added, "Nothing too fancy, because I've got a lot to do."

Bill smacked and rubbed his hands. "I'm going to save room for the turkey. How about you boys?"

Evan, the youngest, said petulantly, "I'm hungry." He sat with his elbows on the table and cradled his chin in his palms.

"How about some corn flakes, honey?" asked Harriet, pulling her robe closer across her front; with her free hand she poured Bill a cup of coffee.

"Corn flakes sounds good to me," said Bill. Then, congeniality muted, he asked, "What about you, son?" to his oldest boy who sat erectly at the table, tee shirt tucked into his jeans, and bare feet flat on the floor. The boy dropped his eyes behind glasses similar to his father's, except that his glasses were held together with a lump of Scotch tape. "I don't care," he said.

"Oh, Billy," said Harriet, "you've hardly eaten a thing since you got home." Frowning, she put her hand on his forehead.

He drew back. "I'm okay."

Harriet peered at the large dark bruise over his left eye. "I think you ought to see Dr. Feldstein about that."

"The skin isn't broken," said his father. "A little football practice never hurt anyone. Right, son?"

"I'm okay," Billy repeated.

"I'm hungry," said Evan.

"Well, get your corn flakes," said Bill. "Your mother's got to get Thanksgiving ready. Okay, hotshot?"

"Is that all we're having?" Evan whined.

"Where's Jo-jo?" Bill asked, cup arrested at his lips.

"I guess he's sleeping late," said Harriet vaguely. "Do you want corn flakes too, Billy?" She was at the cupboard, pulling clattering bowls from the shelf. One was thick cream-colored pottery with a band of sunflowers painted around its rim; in the center of the other was a big yellow smiley face over the legend, "Have a Nice Day!"

"I don't care," said Billy.

"Jo-jo ought to get down here to be with the rest of us," said Bill. Then to Evan, "Why don't you go up and get my camera, son, and wake up Jo-jo while you're up there. Will you do that for daddy?"

With a pained sigh, Evan pushed himself away from the table. He was thin, like his brother, and tall for nine years; reddish-brown hair fell over his ears and forehead. "Where is it?" he asked, aping exasperation.

"It's on the dresser, honey," said Harriet. "I think. Maybe in the top drawer with the guns." From the icebox she took a carton. "I want everyone to drink their orange juice. I want my boys to be healthy." She poured half a water glass and handed it to Bill, then another for Billy. "Drink up, now. Get your vitamin C." She poured herself a cup of coffee.

"What time are they getting here?" Bill asked.

Harriet sighed. "Around five, I guess. That's what Helen said yesterday." To Billy she added, "You will wear your uniform, won't you, honey?"

Jovially, Bill answered for him. "Of course he will, won't you son? Make your mother proud of her college boy?"

Billy sipped his orange juice expressionlessly.

"That bird," said Bill, "has got to be one of the biggest we've ever had."

"Twenty pounds," said Harriet, regarding it distastefully. "I guess I ought to get it stuffed and into the oven."

Evan returned, the camera dangling by its shoulder strap from his hand, and gave it to his father.

"Did you wake up Jo-jo?"

"He's coming down."

Bill backed from the drainboard with the camera to his eye, aimed at the blue-white glistening bird. "I think," he said, "we should all get around the turkey, kinda like it was part of the family. A joke."

Jo-jo, yawning, padded into the kitchen on bare feet; like his brothers he wore jeans and a tee shirt, and was as thin as they. On his upper lip there was a smudge of reluctant moustache. "Ugh," he said, looking at the drainboard, "that's gross."

Harriet said, "Here's your orange juice, honey. You want corn flakes like the rest of the boys?"

"Just coffee."

"You ought to eat breakfast, honey. There's not going to be much for lunch, I can tell you."

"Eat something," said his father.

"I'm not hungry." Jo-jo pushed his touseled brown hair off his narrow forehead, and sniffed, as though he smelled something unpleasant.

"Can I have some toast?" asked Evan.

"Sure, honey," said Harriet. "Anybody else want some toast? How about you Billy?"

"No."

"What do they feed you down there for breakfast? Hog jowls? Grits? Corn pone?" Jo-jo asked.

"Just stuff," said Billy shortly.

"Everything a growing boy needs," said his father. "Right, son?" He glanced at Billy, but his son did not meet his eyes. "Okay, everybody," he said quickly, "let's gather around the turkey for a picture."

"Oh, honey, I look so awful," said Harriet, smoothing her uncombed hair, short and reddish, behind her ears. She pulled her robe closer to her chin and adjusted her silver-framed glasses.

"You look just fine. Doesn't she, boys? You stand over there right next to the old bird." He aimed the camera at the drainboard, and backed further away. "Now Billy go stand next to your mother, and Jo-jo, you get on the other side. . . ."

Billy stood stiffly at his mother's side, his face a blank beneath the short-cropped black hair. Jo-jo rolled his eyes at the ceiling and slouched against the drainboard with exaggerated boredom as he looked into the camera.

"Now, Evan," said Bill, the camera to his eye, "you hunch down in front of the bird . . . there . . . Billy, put your arm around your mother's shoulder . . . get closer to the turkey, Jo-jo . . . no don't hide it . . . Okay now, everybody, here we go . . . smile. . . ." The bulb flashed.

"Honey," Harriet said to Billy, "You're as tall as your father. Have you grown that much in just three months?"

"No," Bill answered for him, "you just didn't notice before. Right, son?"

"Well, one thing's sure," Harriet said, breaking out of the tableau, "you sure are a lot skinnier than when you left here."

"That's exercise," said his father. "It's all muscle."

Billy sat at the table and spooned up a soggy mound of corn flakes.

"What can we do to help, mother?" Bill asked, setting the camera on the table and taking up his coffee.

"Oh, just stay out of the way." She poked the turkey as though she were trying to get its attention. "I guess this thing's ready to go into the oven."

"You want us to peel the spuds, or something?"

"We're having sweet potatoes. I got canned ones." She sighed again.

"Daddy, can we go to the pistol range?" asked Evan.

"It's closed," said Jo-jo.

"We'll go Saturday," said Bill. "Jo-jo, sit up and take your elbows off the table."

Jo-jo remained slumped over his coffee just long enough to establish a doubt as to whether he would comply, then with elaborate weariness sat back in his chair. He looked at the ceiling through half-closed eyes.

Bill carried his cup to the head of the table and sat, facing Billy at the opposite end. "I wonder," he said, "if Jerry Hardin got in last night."

"*He* was supposed to bring me a pennant too," said Evan, looking reproachfully at Billy, who did not appear to notice.

"You'll get your pennant, hotshot, when Billy comes home for Christmas—isn't that right, son?"

Billy's eyes gleamed sullen behind his lenses.

"I don't know," said Harriet, answering Bill as she looked out the window over the sink. "I don't see any extra cars in their driveway. Grace said he might not get in until this morning."

"How come *you* got home so early?" Jo-jo asked Billy.

"It just worked out that way."

"Yeah, but three whole days?"

"I just did."

"Why don't you have Jerry over sometime during the vacation, son?" Bill said. "Maybe he'd like to go to the pistol range with us."

"Grace doesn't like him to fool around with guns," said Harriet.

Bill snorted. "Well, she and Bert can't make a sissy out of him. I bet he'd like to shoot a few rounds. You want to invite him, son?"

"I don't think I'll be seeing much of him."

Bill set his cup down. "You'll see him if you make a point of it."

"We don't run in the same crowd."

"Well, make an effort, son. Just call him and ask him."

"Maybe." Billy stared at his corn flakes.

Jerry Hardin and Billy Johnson were the same age, give or take a month or two, and had lived next door to each other most of their eighteen years. Their parents remained neighborly, even as Bert and Grace Hardin had acquired two cars to every one of Bill and Harriet Johnson's, had painted their house twice as often, had hired a yardman while Bill or his sons mowed the Johnson lawn. Bert was affable, prosperously stout, and alcoholically ruddy; Grace, as their fortunes improved, grew pudgy, but with make-up, dye, hairspray, and an assortment of pants suits, dresses, and coats that ran heavily to primary colors, she acquired the glitter of a new kitchen appliance.

Harriet and Bill watched their neighbors' upward spiral with conventional envy, but without bitterness—"That Bert Hardin is cleaning up," Bill might say, shaking his head, or Harriet might observe, "I'll swear, Grace seems to get a new outfit every time she turns around."

Billy was sure, however, there was one thing the Hardins had that his father, at least, coveted: a popular, handsome, athletic, smart son. Never once had Bill Johnson looked at his own son and said, "I wish you could be like Jerry Hardin," yet it seemed to Billy that his every shortcoming was magnified by the presence, on the other side of the backyard hedge, of a kid next to whom he would always be inadequate.

The awareness had germinated at a neighborhood birthday party where the stout red-headed little Hardin boy had shoved the less robust Johnson boy and made him cry (and, confusingly, it had been Billy who was admonished, not the shover); it took root during a ball game when everybody wanted Jerry on his team, and Billy was finally assigned at the end amid groans from the group that had to accept him; it flourished when Jerry's bright blue eyes remained unsheathed while Billy had to correct a myopic squint with glasses that brought jeers of "four eyes" and "sissy" down on his head.

Billy had recognized at an early age the division between himself and Jerry, but their two fathers behaved as though their sons were the best of friends. They did not appear to understand that though of the same age, and in the same location, the two boys inhabited different worlds: Jerry was the center of a group who gathered around his lustrous prominence, while Billy remained apart, outside the magic shell, attracting no one.

"Why don't you get Jerry and some of your other friends together, and we'll go hiking this weekend?" Bill said when both boys were in grade school.

"I don't want to," Billy mumbled.

"Why not, son?"

"I just don't."

"A boy your age ought to be more active. That little Jerry is on the go every minute. Come on now, I'll call Bert and set something up."

"I don't want to."

"That's silly Billy talking. Straighten up now and behave yourself."

Bill had indeed led them on a hike, with the encouragement of the other boy's parents, and Billy mingled; but though an unstated truce was in effect because of his father's presence, both he and the others knew he remained unabsorbed. All Bill chose to see, from the heights of adulthood, was a group of noisy, racing, roughhousing boys, and he noted with satisfaction that his own son, though perhaps a mite more restrained, was not very different from the others.

One incident, however, scarred the illusion the parents had about their children. For his ninth birthday Bill gave his son a basketball. He made a special trip to the school with it, having taken half a day off from the office, and arrived at the playground during Billy's phys ed class. As he got out of the car, smiling diffidently, with the ball under his arm, the cluster of boys on the asphalt yard watched him curiously. Coach Wynoski, pot-bellied under grey sweat shirt, bulging calves beneath navy blue gym shorts, and a quizzical, not particularly welcoming expression shaded by the brim of his baseball cap, stopped the calisthenics as Bill approached.

"Hi, coach," he said. "I'm Bill Johnson, Billy's dad. I thought I'd drop off his birthday gift here where he can get some use out of it." He bounced the ball twice on the black asphalt. It thumped hollowly in the warm autumn air.

"That's a really keen thing to do," the coach said, polite but annoyed at having his class interrupted. He looked at the group before him; it was early in the school year, and he was not sure which boy the man was talking about. "Where's Billy Johnson," he yelled heartily.

"Here he is," said one of the boys, and gave Billy a shove. Spindly and lanky in his shorts and tee shirt, Billy was propelled to the front of the group, where he stood, gawking at his father and the coach.

"Happy birthday, son," said Bill, and with an extra hard thump bounced the ball to him. Billy caught it awkwardly. Everyone waited for him to do something with it.

Coach Wynoski broke the silence. "That's great. That's great." He looked at his watch. "We still have about 10 minutes, guys. Let's have a pick-up game." He smiled at Bill, one adult to another, conferring a treat. Bill smiled back. "Okay, uh . . . Billy, you pick a team, and Jerry Hardin you pick the other."

"Why, hello, Jerry," said Bill, pleased, "I didn't see you there."

"Hi, Mr. Johnson," said Jerry, managing to sound both respectful and sarcastic, pleasing Bill and his own friends simultaneously.

Jerry gathered his team with masterful briskness. Billy hesitated, grinning out of embarrassment, until Coach Wynoski assigned four reluctant boys who sullenly meandered into his orbit.

The game was short. Jerry captured the ball and dribbled it through lackluster opposition to the hoop affixed to a pole in the asphalt. The coach blew his whistle and declared the hour over, shook Bill's hand, and led his charges to the locker room. Billy hung back.

"Thanks Dad," he said, holding the ball out to Bill.

"Keep it son," said Bill impatiently, "so you and your buddies can play with it after school." He patted Billy's head. "I hope you have a lot of fun with it, son."

After school, Billy still carried the ball, uncertain whether to take it home. As he walked down the long green locker-lined hallway, Jerry Hardin and three of his friends appeared

"Neat gift," one of them, Wally, a fat, blond boy with big teeth, said innocently. Jerry smiled, aloof. "Yeah."

"What kind is it?" Brad asked, plucking the ball from Billy's hands as easily as if it were a ripe fruit. He was thin and taller than the others. "Wilson," he remarked disdainfully, and bounced it twice before passing it underhand to Hal.

Hal wore glasses, but no one ever called him four-eyes. He dribbled the ball on the waxed green marbleized floor, dodging, turning, and feinting. Billy followed. Hal zig-zagged through the door out to the asphalt playground. He threw the ball to Jerry, who insolently banged it nearer and nearer to Billy, hopping around him, daring him to reach for it. Billy did, and Jerry easily bounced beyond his grasp and passed the ball to Brad.

Brad began the same maneuver, slapping the ball to the asphalt, directing it close to Billy, then twirling out of his reach.

The afternoon sun slanted through huge trees at the edge of the schoolyard. Billy shaded his eyes and waited. "How come you're not playing?" Brad asked insolently as he skipped in front of him, crouching and thumping the ball rapidly toward Jerry.

"Maybe you don't like it," said Hal, taking over the ball. "You want to get rid of it?"

"No, I like it."

"Then why don't you play with it?" asked Jerry as he weaved from side to side in front of Hal, trying to get the ball away from him.

Hal veered and dribbled toward Billy and Jerry followed so rapidly that he bumped into him. "Excuse *me*," he said. Billy stepped back, out of their way.

Suddenly Hal twirled and tossed the ball up to the flat roof of the school. They were still an instant, craning their necks upward, then Hal, innocently, said, "Aw, shit."

Jerry and his friends laughed, and Billy nervously smiled.

They looked at him.

"I've got to get it down," he said, not meeting their eyes.

"Hal, you asshole, why'd you do a thing like that?" Jerry asked.

Hal, his eyes wide behind his glasses, made himself look dumb. "Gee, I dunno, coach, it just happened." He hung his head. All save Billy found this hilarious.

"How we gonna get up there?" asked Wally.

They studied the wall with its windows and unadorned bricks that rose to form a small parapet around the flat roof, and laughed again.

"Well, Billy, old boy," said Hal, "looks like you lost your ball."

"He's still got one left."

"Poor old Billy, gotta go through life with one ball."

"Come on, guys," said Billy, trying not to whine. "I gotta get it down."

"I didn't know you could get it up," said Hal.

"There's a ladder on the other side," said Brad. Though it was still light, the sun was behind the trees; other students and teachers had left.

Jerry found the ladder and placed it against the wall, then looked at Billy.

"Well," he said, "there it is."

Billy hesitated. To Hal he said, "You threw it up there. Why don't you go up and get it."

"Why don't you make me."

The others watched, expectant. Billy climbed the ladder, jiggling on each rung, until he got over the edge and onto the solid black tarred roof punctured with silver pipe-chimneys. He found the ball and returned to the edge. Peering over the side he saw the ladder lying on its side against the building, and the boys, laughing up at him.

"Come on you guys," Billy called, "put it back up."

"Like to help you, Billy," Hal yelled, "but we gotta go now." They made an elaborate pantomime of departure, calling "So long!" and waving.

He knew they would not leave him there, but he could not help calling. "Come on, guys. Put the ladder back."

"So long." "Good by." "Be good."

They disappeared around the school, and after a few minutes, Billy ran to the other side and saw, disbelieving, that they really were leaving, walking across the parking lot toward the main road.

"Hey, you guys," he yelled.

They looked back, laughed and waved. Hal jumped up and down and scratched his armpits, imitating an ape.

They'll be back, he thought. He fought to keep his eyes dry, for he did not want them to see tears. He sat, leaning against the parapet, the ball beside him. A breeze raked the roof and made him shiver.

When he stood again and looked out across the parking lot, there was no one. He stared straight down; the asphalt was distant and hard.

He yelled at the top of his voice, "Hey!" In the stillness following his echo he heard cars skimming along the main road.

Twilight, then night obscured the ground, and the chill grew into cold. The automatic ground lights switched on spookily, making him think for a few moments someone had come. He huddled against the parapet, his knees pulled to his chest, and rubbed his bare arms, prickly with goose bumps.

In the silence of the black and moonless night he heard a motor. He ran to the parapet as a car eased into the parking lot.

"Hey!" he yelled. "Hey! Help me!"

"Billy?" It was his father.

"I'm up here," he called, fighting tears of relief.

"Okay, son, hold on." His father approached the wall, found the ladder and lifted it into place. "Can you make it down?"

"Yeah," Billy said and, grasping his basketball, he scampered to the ground that had been so inaccessible minutes before.

"Are you all right, son?" Bill asked, putting his arm around Billy's shoulders, and pulling him close. "Where's your jacket?"

"I didn't bring one," Billy mumbled, grateful for the weight and warmth of his father's arm. He leaned into the solidity of the adult body, as Bill steered him to the car.

The heater was on, and the warmth caressed Billy's bare flesh. His father got in on the driver's side and slammed the door. Instead of starting the car, though, he sat with both hands on the wheel, and stared straight ahead through the windshield. Suddenly he hit the steering wheel and said, "Why did you let this happen, son?"

"I don't know."

"You don't know? If you don't, who does? Your mother's been worried sick. What made you get yourself stranded on that roof?"

"The guys were fooling around . . . and they threw the ball up there."

"Why did you let them?"

"I don't know."

His father snorted. "This was a silly thing for you to do, son."

"I couldn't help it."

Bill turned the ignition. Then he said, "Grace and Bert are going to tan Jerry's hide for the part he played in this. They called me as soon as he told them what had happened. But, son, you should never have let those boys get the best of you."

"I couldn't help it."

Bill said, "Of course you could. You're as big as they are. Let them know you'll knock the hell out of them if they try anything with you." He raced the motor angrily. "You've got to stick up for yourself, son."

Billy's relief froze in his breast. He could taste the next day when everyone would know.

His mother asked whether he had caught cold, or hurt himself. Immediately there was a knock on the front door, and Bill opened it to find Grace and Bert flanking their hangdog son.

"Jerry's come to apologize," Bert said. Sternly, he pushed his son forward by the shoulder.

"I'm sorry," Jerry muttered glumly.

Bill said, "You boys shake hands and forget about it." He pushed Billy towards Jerry. "Shake hands, son."

Billy took Jerry's hand. Their eyes met, then Billy looked away.

Grace clicked her tongue and said, "I swear I don't know what gets into these kids. Bert and me are just as sorry as we can be about this."

"Boys will be boys," said Bill.

"Why don't you all come over for a drink?" said Grace.

"Thanks," said Bill, "but we've got to feed the kids and all. Maybe you'll give us a raincheck?"

"You bet," said Bert. He smiled at Billy and added, "Say, happy birthday, sport."

"Thanks."

Things were strained between the two families for a while; but Bill and Harriet did not hold grudges, and Bert and Grace were affable, and soon the breach closed.

Billy and Jerry were warily polite to each other in front of their parents, but nothing else changed. Jerry's popularity illuminated all who clustered around him. Billy stayed in the shadows, and no one saw his rage.

As he sat at breakfast on Thanksgiving morning, a spoon of corn flakes at his lips, he appeared to be indifference itself.

Harriet opened two cellophane packages of bread cubes and dumped them into a bowl, then, leaning on the counter, read the back of one.

"You're sure there's nothing we can do to help?" Bill asked again.

"Uh-hum," said Harriet. Then, "You could make your own beds, everyone. Straighten up your rooms."

"That's not too much to ask, is it boys?"

Only Evan replied, "Sure."

Billy rinsed his bowl and stacked it in the dishwasher. His father put his hand on his shoulder. "Listen son . . . about last night . . . I'm sorry."

Billy looked at him quickly, expectantly.

"I didn't mean to . . . you know . . . get so carried away. . . ." Bill stood awkwardly just inside the dining room, where the others could not hear. "Listen, everything's going to work out all right. You'll see. By Christmas time you'll think it's the greatest school in the country."

Billy lowered his head.

"Okay, son?"

"I . . ." Billy began.

"You'll see," Bill interrupted. "Everything's going to be all right." He clapped him on the shoulder and went upstairs.

Chapter Two

By THE TIME Bill had showered, shaved, and gotten into his weekend khakis, the odor of sage and
turkey fat wafted through the house. He sniffed and
smiled as he entered the kitchen.

Harriet, still in her robe, the sleeves rolled up,
was bent over the sink, grimly scraping carrots. Bill
put his arms around her waist and said, "It smells
like Thanksgiving."

She smiled and split a carrot down the center.

"It's such a pretty day I think I'll putter around
in the yard a little," said Bill, looking over his wife's
shoulder through the window. The sky blazed blue
and the sunlight on the crackled yellow sill looked
hot.

"Hmmm," said Harriet.

"Anything I can do for you here?"

"No, thanks."

He gave her a hug and went out the back door.

It was very warm. The limbs of the two large old maples at the furthest corners of the backyard were almost bare in the brilliant day. The grass, dry and patchy, retained a hint of green where it showed through the cover of fallen leaves that rustled as Bill, frowning, walked through them. He turned and surveyed the back of the house. The grey asbestos shingles on the lower part seemed to be holding up, but the red trim was blistered and peeling; warily, he scanned the roof and thought, well, at least it *looks* okay.

He kicked through the leaves that had piled up in the narrow passage between the garage and the raggedy privet and yanked up the garage door. It rumbled reluctantly into the ceiling. Standing in the driveway he peered at the jumble surrounding the Ford: tool box, portable barbecue, old trunks, cardboard boxes, green plastic cushions and their folded aluminum frames; rake and hoe handles bristled like dropped weapons. Motes of dust rose in the air and his nostrils flared to the mingled odors of gasoline, oil, and mildew.

Arms akimbo, he peered within for a few seconds, then yanked the dangling strap and stepped back as the door rattled and banged closed.

He turned to the hedge, waist-high along the driveway; in the next yard Bert Hardin, walking with the careful dignity of a man who has learned to tolerate hangovers, was inspecting his own house.

"Happy Thanksgiving," Bill called. "Man, isn't this some beautiful day?"

Bert, portly in a green and tan houndstooth jacket, well-cut short greyish brown hair still damp from the shower, and face glowing red in a simulation of good health, cautiously replied, "Yeah. Same to you, Bill. How's it going?"

"Great. Terrific. Your kid get home okay?"

"Yes. Grace tells me Billy got in last Monday."

"Yeah, some got out early."

"Good, good," said Bert vaguely. "Well, they're growing up."

"Yes. How's Jerry like Penn State?"

"Oh, he's sold on it. Got himself some little gal from New York. We're going to meet her tonight. Going into the city for dinner."

"Great."

Bert nodded affably, his gaze blinkered by attention to his vital signs. "How about you folks?"

"It's going to be a family day. The wife and me and the boys, and Gene and his wife, of course."

"Oh, yes," said Bert blankly.

"Gene's my cousin. I think I've mentioned before. He and I were raised together, and I was just like a big brother to him. His dad was killed in the war, and mine had died before that, so we kinda relied on each other." There was a slight catch in Bill's voice.

"Oh, yes," said Bert again. "Well, that's nice." He smiled pleasantly, his eyes distant.

Looking at the Hardin house, Bill said, "That paint job is sure holding up."

Bert carefully turned the half circle to face his own house. The white clapboard gleamed and the black shutters sparkled as though the paint were wet. A low evergreen hedge outlined the foundation as neatly as an architect's drawing. There were no leaves on the Hardins' smooth, trimmed lawn.

"Yep," he said with a sigh. "It ought to last a couple of years."

"I'm going to get the boys to take care of ours next summer. No use in feeding a houseful of boys if you can't put them to work." Bill laughed. Bert smiled as he speculatively eyed the Johnson house. "Of course, Billy may decide to stay down South."

"Oh, is that right?" asked Bert. "He really likes it down there, huh?"

"Yeah. It's an awfully pretty place."

"Grace said he got kind of bunged up. Or broke his glasses. Or something."

"Football," Bill said quickly. "He was playing football wearing his glasses. I guess they don't teach you everything in college these days."

"Heh, heh," said Bert, rationing his mirth to protect his system.

"How's Jerry doing with his football? He playing any?"

"Oh, yes. He's gonna keep his scholarship."

"Say, that's just great. That's really terrific."

"Yeah, we're proud of him."

"Well, I should think so. I sure hope we get to see him over the holidays."

"You will, you will. As a matter of fact he brought Evan a pennant, or maybe Jo-jo—one of your boys."

"Now isn't that something." Bill's smile was grateful.

"Well," said Bert, "I guess I've done enough work for one day." He winked at Bill. "I told Grace I was going to check up on our yardman."

"He seems to do a pretty good job."

"Ought to for what we pay him, God knows." Bert looked sourly at the lawn. "I think it's time for a little nap before the game starts. You gonna watch?"

"Oh sure. Wouldn't miss it. Good to see you, Bert."

"You too, Bill. We're going to have to get together . . . uh . . . one of these days."

Bill nodded and beamed as Bert, carefully as a damaged ocean liner finding its berth, ambled into his house.

Bill's breast expanded. A good neighbor. Who would have thought, he mused, twenty years ago, I'd be here today, with a house in Beaudale, and neighbors like Bert and Grace. He chuckled ruefully to himself. "I was a sap," he thought. "How could I have been such a sap?" For at first, he'd been against the move.

"We can't *afford* to live in Beaudale," he had said to Harriet when she told him.

"But she's giving us the house," Harriet replied, confused.

He shook his head stubbornly. "You don't understand. There's taxes, and then it's a town . . . well, it's just not a town we can afford . . . I mean everything costs more there. . . ."

In northern New Jersey towns were ranked: Bergen County residents knew, once they learned where a man lived, what his house had cost and what colleges his children stood a chance of getting into. The towns were strung like beads along Kiowa Road, the main thoroughfare that linked them to the larger world. Beaudale was among the most glittering; Ralston, where Bill Johnson had been raised, and where he and Harriet spent their first married years, was dim in comparison.

"Besides," Bill added, "We have our friends here, and Billy will start school soon. . . ."

"We can make friends in Beaudale," said Harriet, still confused, "and the schools there are better than here, everybody says."

Bill shook his head. "It's different for you. That's where you were raised. But I don't know anyone there. They're not the sort of people. . . . I mean, they're different from around here. . . ."

"They're just people," said Harriet reasonably.

Bill sighed and looked at the table. Billy had been fed and was crawling among the debris he had created in the living room. "When is she leaving?"

"Mother? In a couple of months. She's been thinking about it for a long time."

"Why doesn't she just sell the house?"

Harriet was as near to exasperation as she ever got. "She wants us to have it. She doesn't need the money. She asked me if we'd like to live there and I said yes. Honestly, Bill, I don't see why you're acting this way. It's a good house. It's bigger than this one, and, well, it *is* nicer, and in a nicer neighborhood and all. . . ."

He nodded, still looking at the table where the bowl of vividly green, formerly frozen peas had shriveled, each contracted and wrinkled, like tiny aged heads. Pale tan gravy congealed on their plates, and slices of Wonderbread grew stale and stiff on a saucer.

Bill stirred his coffee, even though he had started taking it black. "Velma's a really great person to do this," he said gloomily.

"Well, she doesn't have anyone else, and she's always wanted to go to California, so . . ." Harriet shrugged.

"I'll have to think about it," he said after a while.

How grateful he was now, on Thanksgiving day, after shooting the breeze with his good neighbor, that he had not refused. He walked through the leaves relishing their acrid smell, his chest expanded with the beauty of the light and the purity of the air, and, even more, with the certainty that nothing but nice things were going to happen: his family around him, his wife, his sons, his cousin who was like a brother. Who would have thought, he wondered, not for the first time, that this could happen to me? How lucky can one guy get?

He stopped in the middle of his front yard, and stared at the ground, his toe pushing the leaves backward and forward, his hands in his pocket. As sometimes happened, shards of the past pricked his contentment. "Bastard, bastard, bastard!" Gleeful childish voices reverberated through his memory. "There goes the bastard!"

"But what is a bastard?" Bill had asked, barely able to see over his bowl of oatmeal, petulant and fearful. At one end of the table his mother, in a pale blue nurses' aide uniform, balanced a cup of coffee between her hands, both elbows propped on the worn oilcloth; she did not look at him.

At the other end his aunt Bertha, frowzy and soft, grew flustered and replied, "It's a naughty word, that's what it is." Then, speaking rapidly to his mother she added, "I swear I don't know where kids learn the things they do. Just imagine, Isobel, a bunch of little boys talking like that."

"They hear it from their mothers," Bill's mother replied tonelessly. "They hear their mothers gossip."

His aunt turned on him. "Who were these little snots?"

"Just some kids at school," he mumbled, his head lowered.

"I think I'll just pay a visit to that school," said Bertha.

"Let it be," said his mother, as she set her cup down decisively. "I've got to go. I'll be late." To him she said, "Be good and do what Bertha tells you." Peremptorily she put her hand on his forehead, and to Bertha said, "He doesn't seem to have a fever, but I guess he should stay in."

"Sure. I'll take care of him."

"Thanks, Bertha," his mother said. She shrugged into her black cloth coat and left, after giving him a brisk kiss on the cheek. He sat at the table while Bertha, her lips pursed, cleared it and piled dishes in the sink. "You shouldn't talk in front of your mother that way," she said after a long, disapproving silence.

Bertha and Isobel had always been best friends and Bertha had married Isobel's brother. Shortly after the wedding, Isobel left Ralston to study nursing in New York City; a year later she returned with a child, but no ring, no explanation, and no diploma. Her family had been displeased but not over- whelmed, and had taken care of the boy while she worked. But the grandparents had died within two years after her return, so Bertha had taken little Bill in with her own newly born son, Gene.

At the beginning of World War II, Bertha's hus- band marched off to be killed in Tripoli. Bertha hung a gold star in the window and indulged a quietly histrionic grief and thanked God that at least she

still had her little men—as she called Gene and Bill—
to take care of her.

When he was eighteen Bill attended his mother's
funeral. He stood impassively at the grave, and sup-
ported Bertha as loud sobs convulsed her fat shoulders. He was by then working at the A&P, where
he had started part time while in high school; he
yearned to make something of himself.

Then, as he often said, "Harry Truman put me
through college." The Korean War erupted and Bill
was drafted. He was stationed in Washington, D.C.,
for two uneventful years, and when he was dis-
charged he decided to use the G.I. Bill.

Bertha had been against college: "A bird in hand
. . ." she had said portentiously, referring to the
A&P job which, surprisingly, had been waiting for
him when he got out. None of her family had ever
attended college, and though she approved of it in
the abstract—"Believe me, there's nothing like a
good education"—she distrusted the investment of
time and the uncertainty of the results. Bill had also
been anxious, but he had been bolstered by Eisen-
hower in the White House and the easy optimism
of *The Power of Positive Thinking.* He trudged through
a four-year course in twenty-eight months.

He was married by the time he graduated, another
undertaking Bertha bemoaned. "For *one* thing," she
said, "the wife should *always* be younger than the
husband."

"She's only two years older than me."

"Two years is two years."

Another time:

"Do you know anything about her before you started taking her out? I mean, the kind of life she led . . . ?"

"You mean because she's a model?"

"Well, I don't like to hold anything against a girl just because of her job, but I did read that a lot of those girls keep skinny by becoming dope fiends."

"Harriet doesn't even drink."

"Maybe not where you can see her, but she's awfully thin."

"She diets."

"That's what she tells *you*. . . ."

"Aw, lay off it, mom," Gene said, who always took Bill's side.

Another time:

"She talks kind of snooty, if you ask me."

"She talks like everybody else."

"She sure doesn't want you to forget she and 'Mother' have their own house in Beaudale."

"She just mentioned it. Jesus. What's she supposed to do?"

"She kind of lays it on thick, if you ask me."

"Nobody asked you," said Gene, disgusted.

Bertha attended the wedding in the Beaudale St. John's Episcopal Church and sobbed loudly from midway through the ceremony to the end. The bride wore a powder-blue suit with a full skirt that fell to mid-calf, a little white hat with a veil, white shoes, and an orchid. The groom was in navy blue and sported a white carnation boutonniere. The married couple seemed very happy, and at the reception afterwards, given by the bride's mother at the Beaudale Country Club, they kissed while looking at the camera as both held a knife poised over a three-tiered wedding cake. There was no honeymoon because the groom had to attend classes the following day.

By the time he graduated Bill had a job as an administrator in the parts division in the Newark office of Ford. He thought about moving there, but decided not to. "It's not a place to raise kids," he told his wife.

They rented a house in Ralston that had a backyard and two bedrooms. But one, then almost two years passed and Harriet did not conceive. The marriage became strained, and there were stretches of pained silence where accusations lurked.

Then their first son was born and Bill's pride stamped him physically. He walked with more vigor, and stood straighter, and sucked in the paunch that had begun to form around his middle. He called himself Tarzan; Harriet, Jane; and their son, Boy. He would give the Ape Man's yell when he arrived home from work, and pick his way through the chaos the baby created on the living room floor, heading for the kitchen or backyard or bedroom in search of his mate and child. Harriet laughed wryly, and received his kiss with a smile as she put aside the paperback she was always reading.

"I've got plans for that kid," he would say, "He's got a future."

Then came the move to Beaudale. His first weeks there Bill walked around the old house on Bradford Street, so much bigger than any he had ever lived in, with its rhododendron bushes and Russian olive and ancient trees, and hid his fear, even from Harriet.

"Great people here," he told her heartily. "Salt of the earth." He signed up to plant trees at the shopping mall, joined a committee to raise funds for the library, volunteered to coach a Boy Scout baseball team: "I've got a kid that'll be playing before you know it," he told the other fathers. Before the year was out, he lost the need to feign enthusiasm. "These have got to be the best people in America," he told his wife.

"They're nice people," she replied amiably.

One thing Bill noticed was that everyone seemed to *do* something: on Saturday mornings he would see men and women in gleaming white shorts and knit shirts with tennis racquets in wooden frames heading in pairs or groups to the school courts; men and a few women with golf clubs bristling from expensive-looking cases in the back of their station wagons. No one laughed when someone in riding breeches and jodphurs and even crops and funny little velvet hats came into the supermarket.

"You know, honey, we ought to have a hobby of some sort," he said to Harriet, who was not very enthusiastic.

"I've got enough to do as it is," she said, "what with the house and Billy."

"Yeah, but it might be fun to get out more."

"Well," she said vaguely, "Daddy played golf."

Bill fretted for several months about a hobby. He watched his neighbors carefully, feeling left out on those weekend mornings when they all—or so it seemed to him—sped away to mysterious destinations wearing funny clothes.

Then he met Art Brisnof at a Rotary Club lunch and learned about the National Rifle Association and the Hilltop Pistol Range. Art, who had come to Beaudale only a year before Bill, commuted to New York City where he was a vice president for some vaguely defined import-export business. He was second-generation Polish, and crudely self-made. "No motherfucker ever gave me a hand up," he once told Bill. While Bill was uneasily deferential to the old guard in Beaudale, Art was uneasily abrasive: "These shits think they own me? I got news for them." Then, "Hell, Bill, we could buy most of these suckers at discount."

Bill never did learn whether Art was as well off as he implied, but there was no question he was a good marksman. It was more than sport with Art: "You never know when you gonna have to blast a booger out of your living room some midnight. Gotta watch out for your own." These were sentiments that Bill had grown up with, and hearing a rich New York executive say them made him feel good about himself, his new friend, and his new hobby.

Within six months of meeting Art he had bought a Smith and Wesson Model 13 revolver and a Ruger Security-Six Model 117 handgun. Every chance he got he went to the pistol range, and he became so proficient that even Art was impressed. "Goddamn! Nobody's gonna slip up on you, buddy!"

In the first flush of his enthusiasm, Bill urged everyone to take up the sport. His cousin, Gene, was as enthusiastic as he, and often drove over from Ralston for a Saturday afternoon of shooting. Bill tried to get Harriet to the range, and, dutifully, she did accompany him a couple of times. But she hated the noise and the smell, and pleaded that it was not a good idea to leave Billy so much with the babysitter. Then a year and a half after moving back to Beaudale Harriet was pregnant again.

"Must be the water," Bill joked to Art.

"It takes more than water to pull that off where I come from," said Art nudging him in the ribs. Six months later, Art had left, hurriedly, because of some business trouble. "I've been working with a lot of assholes," was the only explanation he ever offered to Bill. For a while Bill was downcast, but then the Hardins moved in next door, and he found new friends in Bert and Grace. "Wonderful people," he

said to Harriet. "Stable. They'll be around for a
while, you can bet your boots."

"They seem nice," she agreed.

Six years later, when Harriet conceived again, Bill
said, "We sure did slip up this time!" But he was
proud and often talked about his houseful of boys.
"Welcome to the barracks," was one of his greetings.
With friends or neighbors such as Bert, he would
sometimes shake his head and say, "Everyone ought
to have three sons." Then he would add, "They're
noisy, and they eat a lot, but I guess they'll take
care of me in my old age."

He trained his sons, made them work for their
allowances ("Nobody's gonna hand them anything
on a silver platter, and the sooner they learn that,
the better"), and directed toward them a continuous
stream of admonitions: "Sit up at the table." "Don't
pick your nose." "Say yes, sir and yes, ma'am."
Creating sound sons was his preoccupation, and led
him into greater efforts of civic service: he became
a scoutmaster, a volunteer to teach a Red Cross life-
saving course, a weekend football coach—someone
other parents could always count on to watch over
their progeny, as well as his own.

He would shake his head and say to Harriet, "Well,
God knows, it's a lot of work, raising kids right. It's
probably more than some people can take on." Not
to mention the expense. There were times when he
had feared there would be no money for orthodon-

tists, or bicycles, or college—but he had managed
so far.

In spite of the burden Bill sometimes was caught
in a sob of gratitude for his family. His chest would
go hollow and his eyes would mist, and he would
be embraced by a quiet, intense warmth, like a flush,
that never lasted very long, and about which he
never spoke. "God, I'm so lucky," he would think
at such times.

In the bright Thanksgiving morning, as he watched
Bert list into his sparkling black and white house,
he took a deep breath and thought, "God, I'm so
lucky."

Chapter Three

SITTING ON WHAT, until Monday, had been his bed, Jo-jo kept glancing through the window down at where his father and Bert were talking. He sheathed his nervousness with a sullen composure as he creased the small rectangle of rice paper and filled it with crackling dry marijuana.

"Man, are you crazy?" said Billy, who had just come into the room.

Eyes half-closed, Jo-jo insolently licked the long edge of the paper and rolled a lumpy cylinder. Involuntarily he glanced out the window again to where his father still stood with Bert. He caressed the faint haze on his upper lip.

"I do it all the time," he said, with unconvincing detachment.

"Not while you're in my room."

"It's my room now. Or will be again when you go back. My stuff's in here."

Billy looked over his brother's shoulder, through
the window, at their father below.

"Man, if he catches you he'll beat the shit out of
you."

"Fuck him." Jo-jo lit the joint.

"You can smell that stuff from here to downstairs."

"You want a toke?" Jo-jo extended the joint between his thumb and forefinger as he retained the
first puff deep in his lungs.

Billy brushed it aside and stood, irresolute, at the
foot of the bed. Behind him Rod Stewart, spikey
hair and angular satin limbs, gyrated on a poster,
glossy against the matte green wall.

"You better take some," said Jo-jo, exhaling. "You
won't get another chance before old Law and Order
gets here."

"Man, why do you push your luck? You're just
stupid."

Jo-jo sucked in another lungful and looked at his
brother, arrogantly expressionless.

"What did that guy mean yesterday," Billy said,
still truculent, "about you cleaning up at school? Are
you dealing?"

Owlishly, Jo-jo blinked and allowed the corners of
his mouth to ease up in the hint of a weary smile,
before noisily exhaling.

"He's just talking."

"Bullshit. You're dealing."

"Maybe. A little here and there."

"Man, you're stupid. You are fucking up."

Elaborately, Jo-jo slid his hand into the hip pocket of his jeans and retrieved a roll of bills. He flicked it against an open palm while looking at his brother. "I didn't get this by being stupid."

Billy looked from the money to his brother's eyes and then out the window. Quickly Jo-jo's glance followed his as he replaced the money.

"How much you got there?"

Jo-jo shrugged. "Around fifty dollars."

"You mean you're selling the stuff at school. Right out in the open where everyone knows?"

Jo-jo sucked in another lungful.

"Man," Billy continued tensely, "if you don't give a shit about your own reputation you ought to think about the rest of us."

Jo-jo's snorted laugh was augmented by a puff of smoke. "What reputation," he asked scornfully. "His?" He dipped his head toward the window. "Yours?"

Billy's jaw worked and his shoulders stiffened as he glared at his brother. Jo-jo gazed back indifferently, and again extended the joint.

Abruptly Billy looked at the table next to the bed on which a portable record player sat, top covered with unjacketed records. "What'd you do with *my* records," he demanded.

"In the closet."

"I've got some good things. Be careful of them."

Jo-jo shrugged. "Nobody's gonna listen to that opera shit. What's going to happen to them in the closet?"

Billy glanced around the room. "You asshole," he said.

"Man, why don't you come off it," said Jo-jo. "You've been a jerk ever since you got home with that lump on your head. What really happened to your head, anyway?"

Billy touched his forehead and looked out the window. "Football," he muttered.

"My ass," said Jo-jo pleasantly. He reclined against the wall, relaxed and slightly smiling, his eyes half open. Smoke wisped from the soggy, ill-shaped joint pinched between his thumb and forefinger which he amiably extended to his brother.

Billy shook his head. With a sigh, Jo-jo said, "You smoked like a chimney yesterday when we were with the guys."

"We weren't in our own home." Then, abruptly, "Those don't seem like the right kind of guys for you to be running around with."

"Aw, come off it. You sound like him." Jo-jo inclined his head toward the window.

"Well, he's our father."

Billy clenched his hand.

"Jeez." Jo-jo rolled his eyes skyward. "He gives me any shit, you know what I do?" He extended his hand with the index finger pointing straight out and the thumb upright like the hammer of a pistol.

Squinting along the line of his finger, he bent the joint of his thumb. Lazily, he moved his finger toward the window and angled it down to the spot where Bill stood with Bert.

Then, lolling against the wall, he watched his brother with a slight, superior smile. "Hey, man," he said in slow motion, "why don't you wind down. You're too tense. You kind of put the guys off yesterday, even after you smoked. You going to see Wilma?" he asked in an appeasing voice.

Billy sulkily replied, "Yeah."

"That's great."

"Look, I'm sorry I got worked up, but, you know, I am your older brother."

Jo-jo, immune to threats, was just stoned enough to be susceptible to sentimentality. His eyes lost their mockery and his face softened. "Ah, shit, man."

Billy continued, "I really do think those guys yesterday were maybe kind of, you know, not the right kind to hang out with."

"They're just guys."

"Yeah, but, you know, Dad's got some kind of standing here in town, I mean, he's got a name and all, and . . ."

Jo-jo studied the joint which had smouldered to a fraction of an inch and gone out. Carefully he crumpled the remaining marijuana into his palm and brushed it back into the plastic packet. "Yeah, sure," he said.

"And, you know, if you get caught dealing . . .
man that could be the end of everything, like even
the end of college or maybe jail. . . ."

"Who's gonna catch me?"

"You keep fucking up here, *he*'s gonna catch you.
He'd throw you out on your ass, man."

"Let him." Jo-jo slapped his back pocket. "Let
him throw me out. In a couple of years I'll be making
more than him."

"That's the dope talking. Shit. You're just a fifteen-
year-old punk kid."

"There's more where this came from." Jo-jo hit
his hip again.

Billy shook his head, as though anger and frustration were flies to be shooed away.

Evan slammed the door open and rushed into the
room with a blue pennant dangling from his hand.
Triumphantly he grasped two of the angles and
spread it across his chest to show the letters, "Penn
State," appliquéd in white felt. "Look what Jerry
brought me."

Jo-jo calmly studied the pennant an instant before
pronouncing, "That's great."

Billy's eyes were invisible behind the reflection of
his glasses.

"It's bigger than the one from Fairleigh Dickinson.
How big will the one be you bring me?" Evan asked
Billy.

"I don't know."

"I hope it's as big as this."

Billy said nothing.

"Jerry's playing football there," he said. "He said he'd give me a sweatshirt at the end of the year—with Penn State on it. He smokes a pipe." Evan wrinkled his nose and looked knowingly at Jo-jo. "What's that funny smell?"

Jo-jo smiled and waved his hand in front of his face.

Evan rolled his eyes wisely at Billy and back to Jo-jo. "I know what you've been doing."

"Keep it to yourself," said Jo-jo.

"Daddy sure would be mad."

Imitating Evan's voice, Jo-jo said, "Daddy gets mad, I got this for him." Again he extended his finger like a pistol.

Evan giggled, then abruptly asked Billy, "Are you going to bring me a pennant at Christmas?"

"You should have gotten one when you were down there this summer."

"I wasn't collecting them then."

Billy shrugged. "I'll see."

Evan pouted. "You promised."

"Well I fucking forgot!" Billy said through clenched teeth. He wheeled and slammed out of the room.

Chapter Four

HARRIET HAD CHANGED into a beige skirt and nubby russet sweater, run a comb through her hair, and put on some lipstick. She was sitting at the kitchen table, a cup of coffee before her, reading a paperback. She glanced up and smiled when Billy entered.

"You hungry, honey? You can just munch on something, can't you, since we're having dinner so early—that okay?"

Billy sat at the table. "I don't want anything."

Harriet, still not quite focussed on him, held the book open; her smile remained vaguely agreeable. When she saw he was going to stay at the table, she cleared away the butter plate and jelly jars and pressed the book face down, the cover splayed open showing a slender, distressed woman on a cliff, wind whipping her long skirts and golden hair into pretty disarray. "Do you want some coffee?" Harriet asked.

"No." He sat with his elbows on the table, his hands peaked in front of him. The silence was uncomfortable.

"I think you should eat something. I don't care what your father says, I think you've lost some weight."

"I don't want to go back there."

Harriet blinked behind her silver-framed glasses. "You mean to school?"

"Yeah."

"I thought it was an awfully pretty place. . . ."

"I guess, but . . . I don't want to go back."

She let her hand fall on the paperback and ruffled the edges with her thumb. "Well, that's something for you and your father to talk about."

"He won't listen to me. I tried to talk to him, but he doesn't pay any attention."

"Oh, honey, I'm sure that's not right. He wants what's best for you—for all you boys."

Angrily Billy said, "But he doesn't . . . didn't hear what I was saying."

Harriet rose and went to the sink where she fished a cup out of the dishpan, rinsed and filled it with coffee. "Here," she said soothingly.

He clasped the cup with long, thin fingers without raising it, and twirled it in place on the table in front of him. "I tried to talk to him last night, but he kept saying it was all my fault."

"What was your fault?"

"That I didn't like it. That I didn't want to go back."

"Well, honey, you haven't been there very long. You might be a little homesick."

"I'm not homesick," he said vehemently. "I don't fit in there. I made a mistake. *You* made a mistake to send me there."

Harriet looked dismayed. "Now, honey, you talked about that school for a year. You and your dad. You know he wouldn't send you somewhere you didn't want to go."

"I didn't know what it was like. I was wrong."

"You have to give these things time."

"I've been there three months."

Harriet looked around the kitchen and absently smoothed her hair back over her ears. "I've got to do something about this," she said, separating a strand of hair and tugging it before working it back into place. "What with Helen coming and all." Worriedly, she faced Billy. "Your father will work this out." She brightened. "Someday you'll look back and find this funny. Everyone thinks they're at the end of their rope sometimes but they never are. You'll see if I'm right when you're older."

She was relieved to have found the right words.

As a child she had heard, "My what a pretty little girl," echoed among grownups; as she grew older the refrain was complemented by, "Yes, and she's just as sweet as she's pretty."

Her parents, Velma and Harold Hamson, were in their early forties when she, their only child, was born, and they never raised their voices at her. *"Nice girls don't do that,"* her mother might murmur when she was naughty. She was dressed in ruffles and patent leather shoes and her father liked to show her off at his pharmacy, where customers would say, "What a pretty little girl."

Her father died as the Depression settled over the land, but mother and daughter were in no danger: the house was paid for, Harold had left plenty of insurance, and Velma sold the pharmacy for a good price.

"Such a pretty girl," her mother's friends said. "She ought to be in pictures."

"And she's just as sweet as she's pretty," others added. "She's just the best-natured little thing in the world."

As World War II was winding down, she met an air force lieutenant at the USO in Newark where she was a weekend hostess. Tall and laconic, with a little moustache like Robert Taylor's, he was on his way back to Montana. Violating the rules, she allowed him to take her home.

They began to see each other, and Harriet discovered streaks of possessiveness, jealousy, and insecurity in herself. She gave herself to the man out of desperation, hoping to eradicate the unhappiness he had brought into her life. Instead, he made her pregnant.

The lieutenant confessed he had a wife in Montana and could not marry her, but he did not abandon her; he found and paid for an abortion. She confided in no one, and one Friday night rode to a dingy street in Paterson where she was operated on. The lieutenant drove her back to Beaudale and said goodnight. It was the last time she saw him.

For weeks afterwards she was so unlike herself that Velma tried to get her to see a doctor. "I'm all right," she said, and then, uncharacteristically, "Just leave me alone." After a while she recovered, and soon was her pleasant, cheerful self again.

Her mother thought it might be good for her to go to college. Though her grades were not very good, colleges in the postwar boom were not very choosy. Harriet thought about going away, but then the editor of the *Beaudale Journal*, a friend of her father's, entered her in the Miss New Jersey contest. "You're the prettiest girl in the state," he said, and ran a picture of her every two weeks or so. She did not win the contest, but she did get calls from local photographers and clothing stores, and that was how she became a model.

It was fun at first, but when a photographer suggested she make the leap into the big time, go to New York and become a *real* model, she laughed and shook her head.

She met Bill through another Korean War veteran, and she found him pleasant, serious, and quiet. He was somewhat in awe of her—he had never met a model before, he said several times. She had had other boyfriends, certainly, since the lieutenant. She was like a rock in a cluttered river; people flowed past and occasionally one would swirl against her, held by the current of circumstance for a while before sweeping on. Bill adhered, at a time when she was ready to settle down. Her mother thought he was a nice boy. They were married.

The first two years of their marriage were unhappy, like a dead radio. She feared that her abortion, about which Bill knew nothing, had rendered her barren.

Then Billy was born and suddenly the radio made music. Now, when the house was messy, or the meals delayed, there was a reason gurgling or squawling or crawling underfoot. She fed, clothed, and dandled the baby, but it was her husband who undertook to form him. That was fine with Harriet; she countered transgressions with a mild, "I don't think your father's going to like that."

Her second son was christened George, though he was called Jo-jo because that was how Billy said his name. Evan came. As the boys grew older, Harriet was left with more time on her hands. She sewed some, and read constantly, mostly paperbacks with glossy covers that showed breathless women in moments of tension.

"My wife's a great reader," Bill said, when someone came across one of the books strewn around the house. "Always has her nose in a book."

Harriet laughed and said, "It's something to do."
When Evan started school Bill worried that she might become restless with so much leisure. After a while it seemed easier to placate him than to find excuses. She joined a gardening club and volunteered for the St. John's Episcopal Church charities.

As her sons grew older they became more complicated. Billy did not seem to get on well with other children; Jo-jo was gregarious but wild. She acknowledged the problems, but did not grapple with them, for that was Bill's province. She never disputed his decisions. Bill often told her she was a wonderful wife and mother.

Now her oldest son sat at the kitchen table, hostile; in some peculiar way he blamed her for a misery she could not understand. A turkey sizzled in the oven, and there were cans of sweet potatoes and cranberry sauce and packages of marshmallows to be opened and a jello salad that had to be fixed if it was going to jell in time. Gene and Helen were due at five, her hair was a mess, and so was the house. She smiled vaguely at Billy and repeated, "Everything's going to work out, honey. You'll see." Bolstered, she got heavily to her feet and, clearing a space on the counter by moving the boxes with the mince pies, bought the night before, she fumbled through the stash of pots and pans under the sink until she found one to boil water in.

Billy stared straight ahead.

As Harriet ripped open boxes of lime Jello she said, "You'll wear your uniform for dinner, won't you? We've never seen you in it, honey."

"Yeah."

Harriet smiled and put her hand on his shoulder. "Is that bump on your head bothering you? Does it hurt?"

"No."

Gingerly she touched it, and he reared back, not looking at her.

"I still think we ought to get the doctor to look at it tomorrow."

"It's okay."

"When will your new glasses be ready?"

"Monday."

"They going to send them to you?"

Mutely he looked at her.

She turned away. "I swear, you boys. You shouldn't be playing so rough with your glasses on."

He said nothing.

"What are you going to do now?"

"I don't know."

"Remember, dinner's at five." She sighed and began to search for a can opener.

Billy sat a few minutes longer, his narrow shoulders rigid under the white tee shirt. Then he pushed himself away from the table and went out the back door into the brilliant morning.

Chapter Five

By FOUR-THIRTY, Harriet had changed into a rust-colored wool dress she had made the year before, following a Butterick pattern. It was a simple sheath, unbelted, with a yoke neck and three-quarter sleeves. She liked it because it hid the ridge around her middle.

She set the table in the dining room before straightening up the living room. "Just a lick and a promise," she said as she plumped pillows on the worn sofa, and arranged a pile of paperbacks at one end of the ring-scarred coffee table. At the other end was a round red leather box of coasters which no one ever used, next to a box of Kleenex in a brown floral designer package, one amber tissue jerked to attention.

"The place looks fine to me, honey," Bill told her from his Barca lounger where he was watching the game. "Why don't you rest a little before they get here?"

"Oh," she said vaguely, searching the room for the most salient disorder, "what with Helen coming. . . ."

"Um . . ." Bill looked uneasy. Then, for the fourth time that day he said, "Boy, it sure *smells* like Thanksgiving around here."

Harriet smiled and nodded. She flicked the rag over the end tables and the TV, glanced around the room and, raising her eyebrows in wry resignation, sighed, "I guess this'll have to do."

Bill got up and put his arm around her waist and nuzzled her neck, whispering, "My baby's been working too hard," in a little boy voice. Harriet smiled and scrunched her shoulders. "I guess I ought to spray some Fantastic on that," she said looking at the light switch by the door; the cream wall around it was smudged with fingerprints.

"Leave it," said Bill, still holding her. "Let's just sit down together and relax a little before they get here. Okay?" He nuzzled her again.

She patted his hand. "I've got to put this away," she said, flourishing the dust rag. "And look at the turkey. I never can remember how long the things have to stay in the oven." She gently disengaged herself and went back to the kitchen.

He sat back down in the reclining chair and stared at the screen.

Evan, his hair watercombed over his forehead, wearing a blue and red striped tie—the only one he owned—and a checked shirt, came into the room and leaned against his father. Bill put his arm around his waist as they both stared at the screen. "It's a great game, eh son?"

"Yeah," said Evan.

Jo-jo, red knit tie so loosely knotted that the top button of his collar showed, plopped down on the sofa, his eyes on the screen.

Bill glanced at him. "Fix your tie, son."

Without taking his eyes off the screen Jo-jo slouched against the couch and gave a yank to the shorter end of the tie which, like a drawstring, puckered the neck of his shirt. The three males sat mesmerized by the flickering images as an announcer excitedly told them what they were seeing.

"Anybody home?" Gene called from the front door, opening it without knocking and barging into the living room. His tan bald head gleamed in a nest of black fringe, and his large hands were extended in greeting. A one-piece brown leisure suit was zipped open to expose a chest covered with black hair and festooned with two gold chains. Full lips were topped by a black moustache, and his eyebrows bushed above large brown eyes. "We could have wiped you folks out. Surprise attack. That right, babe?"

He threw the question over his shoulder to a tiny woman whose golden hair was teased and sprayed into a casque that overwhelmed her small face. On the ridges where her eyebrows had once grown, artful brown lines had been pencilled. Her narrow lips were brilliantly red, and a startling blue eyeshadow highlighted the blue of her eyes, which were hard and assessing. Her thin frame was draped in a cherry red pants suit, and with one hand she clutched a black patent leather purse. In the other she dangled a white pastry box by the string securing it.

"That's right," she answered her husband, "we could have had the place surrounded and you wouldn't have known it until it was too late." Her laugh was high pitched and did not touch her eyes.

Bill jumped out of the lounger and the two men collided in a shoulder-thumping embrace. "Well, by golly, Happy Thanksgiving."

"I'm telling you," Gene continued, "you folks better get a good watch dog. How're you boys?" he asked Evan and Jo-jo.

Simultaneously Bill asked "How're things going?"

Gene answered, "As well as could be expected with that son of a bitch in the White House. 'I'll never lie to you,' " he mimicked in a broad Southern accent.

"Ha, ha," said his wife with heavy irony through pinched lips, shaking her golden orb of hair.

Bill also shook his head. Gene turned to the television.

"Who's winning? I've got money on this game."

"Helen," Bill said, "you get prettier every time I see you."

She crinkled her eyes and lips in a laugh. "I just get older."

"She's still the same size she was when we got married," boasted Gene, his eyes on the screen.

"I try to take care of myself."

"Well, it shows." Gingerly, Bill hugged her, and she held out the bakery box to him. "What's this?"

"Oh, just a little something. . . ."

"You folks shouldn't have. . . ." He held the box as she had, dangling by its string, and called, "Honey, come out and see who's here."

"Come and see what the cat drug in," yelled Gene.

"She's been in the kitchen all day," said Bill.

"Oh, my," said Helen.

Harriet came smiling into the living room. "Well, hi!" she said as she and Helen kissed the air beside each other's ears. "How pretty!" she added, motioning to Helen's hair.

"I had one of the girls at the shop do it yesterday." Helen owned and ran her own beauty shop, the Nefertiti, which had a replica of the long-necked Egyptian queen in its window. Ralston men gleefully declared that their mothers, girl friends or wives were getting fixed up at the "Titty."

"How did you get it to stay that way overnight?" Jo-jo asked. "Did you sleep sitting up?"

Helen, startled, laughed hesitantly and self-consciously patted the back of her neck.

Bill glared at his son, who, still slouching on the sofa, met his eyes innocently.

"How are you boys getting along?" Helen asked primly. Then focussing on Evan, she added, "How's school coming, young man?" Before giving him the chance to answer she said to Bill, "My goodness but they grow so quick, don't they?"

"They eat a lot. It costs me a fortune to feed these kids."

"Huh," Gene said, still watching the television, "you think kids cost a lot, you ought to try raising Dobermans. Those babies eat forty-fifty dollars a week—and that's just for the dry food."

"Dinner's going to be a little while," said Harriet, still smiling. "Would you like a little drink?"

"Not me," said Helen quickly.

"Say, that's an idea," Bill said, grinning at Gene.

"I could go for a little something," Gene agreed.

"Honey, why don't you mix them," said Harriet, turning back to the kitchen.

"I'll help you set the table," said Helen briskly.

"The table's all set. Why don't you just relax out here with the men while I get things together."

"No, no, I hear you've been stuck in that kitchen all day, so I'm going to help you out."

"Look what Helen and Gene brought," Bill said, extending the pastry box to Harriet.

"Oh, isn't that nice. Thank you." With forced cheerfulness, Harriet led the way to the kitchen, while Gene sank into the lounger in front of the television.

"You boys holding your own?" he asked, looking at the screen.

"Holding our own what?" asked Jo-jo. Evan giggled.

Gene paused an instant before emitting a half-hearted chuckle.

Although he and Helen routinely complained about their lack of offspring, and even though they were firm believers in the sanctity of the family, and strongly opposed abortion, they cherished their liberty.

Gene had three plumbers working for him who called him "Gene" or "Sir" depending on his mood. Helen was a Ralston girl who had taken a beautician course in New York City but returned home to nurse her father who had leukemia. When he finally died, she bought the beauty shop with his insurance money and made it thrive.

She and Gene found that they made a damned good team. They kept separate checking accounts, but joint savings. Behind their house Doberman pinschers, enclosed by a chain-link fence, loped about like a tankful of barking sharks.

Though they voted, they loathed the Democrats and did not much like Republicans. Helen had no family and Gene's closest relative was Bill, for whom he expressed a tenderness bordering on the saccharine. He would say, "That man is like a brother to me. Hell, he's closer to me than any brother could be." Helen would add, "There's nothing like family."

Gene's feelings splashed onto all of Bill's family, and
he would declare that Harriet was one hell of a wife
and mother, and that Bill's kids were smart little
fuckers. When actually confronted with them, however, he was uneasy. There was something guarded
and withdrawn about Harriet. The three boys were
unpredictable at best, and the little asshole slouching
on the couch was an out and out smart alec. Gene
concentrated on the football game.

Bill returned with two highballs. "I made them
kind of weak, because we're having wine with dinner."

"You want your chair back?"

"No, no, you stay there. How's it going?" They
both watched the screen.

"Well, unless they get off their asses it looks like
I lost twenty bucks."

Bill clicked his tongue sympathetically.

"I'm hungry," said Evan.

"You're always hungry," Bill replied, smiling at
Gene.

"When we going to eat?"

"Soon. Go ask your mother." To Gene, "You
want some carrots or celery—something to nibble?"

"No. This is fine. Where's Billy?"

"He'll be down in a minute. I guess he's in his
room. . . . Is he in his room, son?" he asked Evan.

"I don't know."

"Yeah," said Jo-jo; he was slumped on the couch
with one long leg thrown over its arm.

"Sit up straight, son," said Bill, "and fix your tie. That's no way to wear a tie."

"Why do I have to wear a tie anyway?"

"For Thanksgiving."

"He isn't wearing one." Jo-jo pointed to Gene, who continued to stare at the screen.

Bill's lips compressed. "That's about enough out of you, George. Now sit up straight and fix your tie." Embarrassed, Bill shook his head, glancing quickly at Gene, who pretended to notice nothing.

Helen entered with a plate of carrot and celery sticks and olives in one hand, and a half-eaten stalk of celery in the other. "Here's something to hold you boys till we get everything on the table," she said chirpily. Setting the plate on the coffee table, she watched the screen with an air of informed concern, hand on her hip.

Harriet appeared at the door and announced cheerfully, "It won't be long now." She dried her hands on her red and white checked apron.

"What do you want me to do?" Helen asked.

"Nothing. You just relax in here with the men. All I have. . . ." She stopped in mid-sentence, and her eyes widened. "Oh, honey," she said, looking at the stairs.

The others glanced from the screen toward the living room door, just as Billy stepped into the room.

He seemed to have been caught in a shaft of light. Straight, tall, and thin, he stood at the doorway, the blue of his tight waist-length jacket as deep as mid-

night, the white of his creased, spotless trousers
dazzling. Brass buttons gleamed across his chest,
which, along with his shoulders, seemed to have
broadened, their width and breadth accented by the
narrowness of his waist. He was diffidently aloof, like
a gracious visitor to a charity ward.

"Hi, Gene," he said, nodding. "Helen."

"Oh, honey," said his mother. "You are so *handsome!*" She took his arm flirtatiously.

"By golly," said Bill, "now isn't that something.
What do you think of that? I think we better get a
picture of this. Yes, sir. Evan, run get daddy's
camera."

"Well, well," said Gene. He rose self-consciously
and extended his hand.

"My goodness," said Helen primly, "you've become a regular warrior. What happened to your
head?"

Billy touched the bruise on his forehead. "An
accident," he said.

"They play kinda rough down there," said Bill
jocularly, beaming at Gene and Helen. "Ole Billy
here tangled with some rebel football players."

"You get that playing football?" asked Gene ad-
miringly.

"With his glasses on!" said Bill gleefully, pointing
to the scotch-taped frame.

"Well, I guess you had to see where the ball was,"
said Gene, standing awkwardly, like someone waiting
for permission to sit.

Evan returned with the camera and gave it to Bill, who took charge of the group. "I think I'll have you all in front of the sofa there. Billy, you stand in the middle and honey, you stand beside him. . . ." The flashbulb popped as they smiled, blinked, grimaced, and stared.

"I think we better eat," said Harriet. "It'll be ready in a few minutes."

"I'll help get it on the table," said Helen, heading with determination for the kitchen. Gene reclaimed the lounger and Evan and Jo-jo sank back on the sofa. Bill and his oldest son stood behind the chair watching the screen. Billy seemed to be at attention, back inflexible, shoulders squared.

When Harriet appeared at the door and announced, "I hope you boys are hungry," Bill said, "I think we could eat a little something." He laughed and put his arm around his son's shoulder.

"You bet," said Gene, though he rose with his eyes still fixed on the screen, like someone walking reluctantly away from an old friend.

At the dining room door, Bill said, "Oh, mother. You've really outdone yourself this time." He looked at the white cloth, the lighted candles, and the small bunch of yellow chrysanthemums in a glass bowl in the center. At one end the turkey steamed, dressing bulging from its cavity. A blob of browned marshmallows covered the baking dish of sweet potatoes, and beside it shimmered green Jello salad flecked with carrots and canned white grapes. There was a bowl of gravy, and two baskets of hot rolls, and celery and carrot sticks with olives. All the plates matched—they were the good china, left by Velma when she gave them the house—and the glasses were stemmed and sparkling. On each white plate a large soft paper napkin had been folded into a peak.

"Everybody sit down. I want to get a picture of this," Bill said, returning to the living room for his camera.

"Where do you want me to sit, Harriet?" asked Gene. "Man, this looks like something in a magazine, doesn't it, sweetheart?"

"It's very nice," said Helen primly.

"Oh, anywhere . . . why not there," said Harriet, pointing to a chair. "I want Billy to sit next to me." She smiled at him. "Everybody sit down, now," she added, glancing around the table. "Oh. I forgot the butter." She went back into the kitchen.

"Come on and take your place, mother," said Bill, who stood at the head of the table with the camera at his eye. He backed away until he got everyone into focus. "Come on," he called, impatient, as Harriet returned. Billy held her chair, solemnly pushing it in after she was seated, and then took his own seat beside her. Like everyone else, he turned toward Bill, who snapped them.

"This is a real Thanksgiving," Bill said, beaming above the camera.

"You can say that again," said Gene.

"This is a real Thanksgiving," said Jo-jo mechanically. Evan giggled, but the others ignored him.

"I think," Bill said, suddenly growing serious, "that I'll ask Billy to say grace."

They looked down at their plates as Billy, after an embarrassed hesitation, rapidly intoned, "Oh God we thank thee for this thy bounty and for your blessings, for ever and ever. Amen."

"Amen," they all repeated.

"And I just want to add to that," said Bill, picking up the carving knife, "that I thank the Lord for my family." He flushed slightly. "Gene, why don't you pour the wine while I take care of this big bird."

Gene lifted the elongated bottle beside him and squinted at the label in a half-joking manner.

"I opened it in the kitchen," said Harriet. "I had it in the icebox."

"White for fish and fowl," said Bill, chiseling at the side of the turkey with what appeared to be a dull knife. The flesh came away in ragged chunks. "Who wants white meat?"

"I do," said Helen. "It's less fattening."

"She's still the same weight she was when I married her," said Gene, pouring into Harriet's glass.

"Just half a glass for me," said Harriet.

"Can I have some wine?" asked Evan.

"No," said Bill, "you boys are too young." He paused in his carving and looked at his eldest son. "Billy can have some, though."

Gene laughed and reached across the table for Billy's glass. "I bet this isn't the first little nip he's had." He winked broadly at Billy and asked, "How's the beer down there?"

"Okay."

Bill and Gene laughed; Jo-jo caught Billy's eyes and rolled his own upward.

"I left ole Billy in pretty good hands down there from that point of view," said Bill, still peeling slivers off the carcass. "What's the name of your buddy?" He paused, knife in mid-air. "A good-looking guy."

Billy flushed but said nothing.

"Oh, yes," said Harriet. "Such beautiful manners. A real Southern gentleman. Ernest!" she exclaimed. "His name was Ernest."

"Ernest Jackson," said Bill, resuming his carving. "A really terrific kid. You haven't mentioned him. How is he?"

"Okay."

"You should see that kid," Bill said to Gene. "Poise and looks and smart too. That's what they turn out down there. He took a shine to ole Billy."

"Is that a fact?" asked Gene.

Billy nodded.

"Well, we need all the friends we can get," said Gene.

"Everybody help yourselves," said Harriet, as Bill passed the plates with turkey on them around the table. "Jo-jo, why don't you start the sweet potatoes."

"Everything looks so good," said Gene heartily.

"Oh yes," Helen agreed with markedly less enthusiasm. She sat straight, her tiny painted mouth squeezed into a small smile, and took a spoonful of sweet potato from the dish. Carefully, she scraped off the blob of melted marshmallow clinging to the top and pushed it distastefully to the edge of her plate.

"I'm afraid the stuffing might be a little dry . . ." said Harriet.

"It's just right," said Gene, "isn't it, babe?"

"Perfect," said Helen. She shoved the mound of it on her plate next to the exiled marshmallow.

"I wanted the drumstick," said Jo-jo, looking disdainfully at the slice of thigh on his plate.

"Me too," said Evan.

"When you got a houseful of boys," Bill said to Gene, "you gotta raise turkeys with four legs." Then to his sons: "The drumsticks are too big for one person."

"Not for me," said Jo-jo. "I don't want any of the rest of this glop."

"That's about enough out of you," said Bill sternly.

Gene and Helen kept their eyes lowered.

"Put some gravy on it, if it's too dry," said Harriet, vaguely. She seemed to be referring to the whole meal. "Billy, why don't you start the rolls?"

"Well," said Bill, settling into his chair and picking up his napkin, "this is a real feast." He lifted his glass toward Harriet. "Mother, here's to you."

Billy, Gene, and Helen raised their glasses self-consciously before sipping.

After a lull, punctuated by the clink and scrape of cutlery, Gene swallowed a mouthful of wine and asked Billy, "What you been doing since you got back? You seen that little girl over in Perryville?"

"There've been a lot of phone calls," said Bill, winking.

Everyone looked at Billy. "Not yet," he said. As though to apologize, he added, "She's been studying, and her mother didn't want her to go out just before the holidays. I'll see her tomorrow."

"Such a nice girl," said Harriet.

"Her father's a psychiatrist," said Bill.

"Is he Jewish?" asked Gene.

"No . . . no. Name's Sheffield."

"They could've changed it. Happens a lot."

"No, I'm pretty sure they're not Jews."

"He's a psychologist," said Billy, "not a psychiatrist."

"They seem awfully nice," said Harriet. "I've never met them, but I did talk to the mother once over the phone . . . what's her name?"

"Betty," said Billy.

"That's right. She has a Southern accent."

"Texas," said Billy.

"Oh, she's from Texas." Gene seemed reassured. "So you got a little girl friend here. Bet you got one down there, too. That right?" He smiled at Bill.

"No."

"Why not? You been down there almost three months already."

"I just don't."

"Well, you'll have one by Christmas."

"It's not. . . . I don't have the time." Billy looked quickly at his father.

"They keep him pretty busy down there. It's not one of those pushover schools—no country club, you know," said Bill.

"Anything else would be a waste of money," said Gene.

Both men nodded and Helen said, "I think there's nothing like a good education."

"Helen, here, is taking a course."

"That right?" Bill asked. Helen demurely jabbed at her plate.

"Yeah. Some meditation course."

"TM," said Helen. "Transcendental Meditation."

"Oh." Bill seemed at a loss.

"Isn't that interesting," said Harriet.

"Yes, it is," replied Helen firmly. "It's made me much more aware of myself, of my inner nature."

A strained silence followed, broken by Harriet's query whether anyone wanted anything else. Everyone was full, but yes, they all, except Helen, could eat a little pie with their coffee.

Afterwards the men returned to the living room, where the television, like some forgotten, garrulous guest, droned on. Jo-jo and Evan went to their rooms, and Billy sat, resplendent in his uniform, on the sofa next to his father, keeping his back straight.

"Well, this is living," said Bill. "It's not gonna get much better than this."

"You can say that again," Gene agreed, watching the screen.

After a while, Bill cleared his throat. "You know, when we were kids, we never for a moment thought we'd be this lucky, did we?" Shyly, he glanced at Gene.

Gene kept his eyes on the screen. "No. But, hell, we deserve it. We've worked our butts off." Then, suddenly he barked a laugh. "You remember that girl I was supposed to have knocked up back when you were at the A&P, and how you went to her father and told him if she didn't lay off you'd get the whole check-out staff to swear they'd banged her?" He glanced at Billy. "We weren't always a couple of old farts," he said.

Bill laughed, embarrassed. "Those were the days."

"Hell," Gene said, "you weren't any saint. I remember how you told me you got laid the first time in the army. Down there in Washington."

Bill blushed as he laughed. He looked quickly at his son. Gene caught the look and said, "Ole Billy, here, 's old enough to know about the birds and bees and bimbos. That right?"

Billy smiled and nodded, his eyes on the screen.

Gene reached over and smacked Billy on the knee. "You get any shooting in down there?"

"No."

"They keep a tight rein on the freshmen down there. Won't even let 'em have a car," said Bill proudly.

"That right?"

Billy nodded again.

After a while Helen and Harriet joined them.

"You girls all finished?" asked Gene.

"We just stacked the dishes. I'll wash them later," said Harriet.

Helen smiled sourly to convey her disapproval of unwashed dishes. "Well," she said after a minute, "I guess we ought to get back. I want to check on Maxine." To Harriet she confided, one woman to another, "Maxine's going to litter any day now."

"How nice," said Harriet, who hated Doberman pinschers.

"Yeah," chimed in Gene, "we gonna have some more pups. Talk about eat!" He heaved himself to his feet. After they were in their coats and on their way out, Gene said to Billy, "I want you to go back down there and wallop that rebel that kicked your head." He and Bill laughed, and Billy smiled, his eyes on the floor.

As the motor whined out of the drive, Harriet flopped on the couch, and said, "Well, that's over."

"Mother," said Bill, reclaiming his lounger, "you did us all proud. Isn't that right, son?"

"Yeah."

Harriet picked up the paperback that was splayed open on the coffee table and sat on the sofa. "I think I'll leave the dishes until tomorrow."

The two men watched the screen in silence for a few minutes before Bill suddenly asked, "Where are the boys?"

"Jo-jo went out, I think," said Harriet, not looking up. Bill's lips thinned. As though to compensate, she added, "Evan's in his room trying to decide where to hang his pennant."

Grateful for an excuse to recapture his cheerfulness, Bill said, "That was nice of Jerry. A damned nice kid."

"Grace said he likes his school."

There was canned laughter from the television, but Billy missed the joke. "I liked mine too, at first."

Bill frowned. Harriet lifted her head apprehensively.

Stubbornly, Billy repeated, "I liked mine, too. But it didn't work out."

"But, honey, you just got there," said Harriet.

Furiously Billy turned on her. "I've been there long enough. I'm the one who's there, not you. You're stupid to keep telling me I just got there."

"Don't talk to your mother that way," said Bill, creaking the recliner into sitting position.

Billy looked back at the screen, his closed lips working nervously, as his parents stared at him. "I can't go back," he said to the television set.

Harriet closed her book. "Well, this is something I think you boys had better straighten out between you." She got up, wounded but dignified. "Good night."

Billy muttered, "Good night," without looking at her.

There was more laughter from the television set, but neither father nor son followed the program. "Now, what is this?" Bill asked reasonably.

"I *told* you," said Billy, looking at his father.

"Don't be silly. We've bought your uniforms and paid your tuition. My God, son, do you know what we've spent?"

"I can't help it."

Bill set his lips into a grim line. "Yes, you can help it. You will help it. You can at least stay the year."

"I can't go back."

"What do you mean you can't go back? What did you do? Did you get kicked out?"

"No."

"Tell me the truth, son."

"No, I didn't get kicked out."

"I'm going to call them and get to the bottom of this."

"There's nothing to get to the bottom of. They don't like me. I don't fit in."

"Who doesn't like you?"

"I told you. The . . . guys. The other guys."

"The other students?"

"I told you." Billy's lips quivered and he squeezed his eyes shut an instant. "I hate it there. They hate me. I don't fit in."

"You can't just hop off to another school. I've got two more kids beside you, Billy. They've got to go to college. I can't allow you to just pick up and leave because you think you're not popular. All your life you've refused to get along with people. It's got to stop now. Surely you can see that? You're old enough to understand that."

"I don't need to go to another school."

"What?"

"I don't have to go to college. I could get a job . . . in a garage, somewhere, or. . . ."

Bill slapped him so hard his son's glasses flew against the back of the sofa. "I didn't raise you to become a grease monkey!" he said through gritted teeth. Instantly his expression dissolved like warm wax. He looked away, ashamed. His voice, though, did not catch up with his features, and he harshly added, "You're not going to become one of those dropout bums."

Billy kept his head lowered as he groped for his glasses and fumbled them onto his nose. There were tears at the corners of his eyes.

"You can't just think of yourself," Bill said, but his tone had degenerated into embarrassed self-righteousness. "God knows, nobody paid for my college." Humiliated, he stood and looked at his son. His rage, like a twisted rubber band, had unwound and lay limp within him. "Now you can just get this nonsense out of your head. The very least you can do is finish the year. That's not asking too much, is it?" He tried for sarcasm but sounded plaintive. "Is it?" he repeated more forcefully. "Good God, that's the least you can do for your mother and me."

Billy did not look at his father.

"I don't think I'm being unreasonable," his father said, trying to erase the slap, but too ashamed to apologize. "I—your mother and me, we just want what's best for you, son." He put his hand on Billy's shoulder.

Billy did not look up.

Bill tightened his grip on his son's shoulder, squeezed it twice, standing over him, looking down on the bowed head. "Everything," he said, "is going to work out. You'll see. Everything's going to be okay." He squeezed again. "Okay?"

Billy said nothing.

Chapter Six

THE AUTUMN SUN blazing through the window quickened Billy. He blinked against the glare and myopically looked at his watch: ten o'clock. He stretched, damp from heat, turning a catalog of things to do through his mind; only the Sheffields mattered.

He thought of them as the Sheffields, but he hardly ever saw the husband or the older daughter. It was Wilma and her mother, Betty, who were the Sheffields, and it was Betty whose image sparked anticipation.

He had called the day he arrived, and now he smiled as he remembered the twangy, excited voice: "Billy! Is that you? You calling from school?" Betty Sheffield sounded younger than her daughter.

"No," he replied. "I, uh, got home early."

"Terrific! When you coming over to see us? Wilma can not, I repeat *not*, go out before the holidays because she has a math test the day before, and she is absolutely going to pass it, so that young lady has to study . . ." she broke off, laughing, as, in the background he could hear Wilma say, "Mother . . ." Betty talked faster, "but I can tell you we will be *very* disappointed if we don't see you before you go back. . . ."

"Yeah, I was hoping to get over. . . ."

"Billy?" Wilma said, her voice softer than her mother's. She sounded even more shy than she was.

"Hi."

"Hi. You home early?"

"Well, yeah, some of the guys got out early."

"You like it? I liked your letters."

"Yeah, sure. Thanks for yours."

"How long you here for? Going back Sunday?"

Billy paused. "Yeah, I guess."

Wilma giggled, "You guess."

They were silent an instant, uncertain. "Maybe I can see you after the test," Billy said, "that is, maybe on Thanksgiving?"

"We're going to my grandmother's in Fort Lee for Thanksgiving and won't be back very early. . . . Mother!" she called, "when will we get back from Grandma's?"

He heard Betty laugh in the background, and say, "You know as much as I do about that. It all depends." A hand was put over the speaker.

"It'll be too late," Wilma said. "But maybe Friday?"

"Yeah, sure."

"Just a second, Mother wants to speak to you," and before he could say anything Betty was back on the phone, her voice swooping upward with eagerness, "Billy? How do you like it there? They treating you okay?"

He hesitated.

"Billy? You there?"

"Yeah. I . . ." He was ashamed. Instantly Betty's voice was serious.

"I want to hear all about that place. Why don't you come a little early on Friday and we can have a talk?"

"Yeah, sure," he said, uneasy with the intimacy, yet flattered.

He stretched in the warm morning, blinking against the brilliant rectangle of his window. He decided he would work on his car to kill time until he went to the Sheffields.

In the kitchen his mother read a paperback amid the debris of earlier breakfasts.

"Sleepyhead," she greeted him.

Billy, constrained, mumbled, "Good morning."

"You're the last one up," Harriet continued lightly, with no sign of rancor. "Evan and Jo-jo are out and about and your father is planting trees behind the library." She pressed the book face down on the table and went to the stove. "I made pancakes," she said brightly, "to fatten you up. How many can you eat?"

"Two or three."

"Your father said that if you wanted to join him and the other men over at the library, you could." The batter hissed as she poured it into the skillet.

"I don't think so."

She nodded, her attention on the pancakes. "I wish they could have given you your new glasses right away, instead of sending them. You need anything else before you go back? How's your underwear and socks and things like that holding up?"

"Okay."

"Good." She flipped the pancakes onto a plate and set it before him. "Eat these up and I'll fix some more."

"This is enough."

She looked doubtful, but sat down without protesting. "What are you going to do today?"

"Work on my car, I guess. See Wilma."

"That's nice."

She smiled. "You having a good vacation?"

Looking at his plate, he said, "Yeah."

"Good. Have fun, honey," she said, pleased.

After breakfast he went to the 1969 Cobra that sat, gleaming black and sleek, in the driveway. He stroked the length of it, metal heated by the sun, as he inspected the finish. When he had learned he would not be able to have a car at school, his father

urged him to sell it. Billy was horrified; he would
rather have sold Evan.

A year before Billy had first gaped incredulously
into the motor. "It's your car, son," his father had
said, "and your responsibility." Nothing had a name;
squares, circles, rectangles, cubes—all greasy black
and linked by tubes, fat and narrow, smooth and
pleated, that meandered among them. Hovering
above the chaos like a flying saucer was a round,
lidded frying pan with a handle. Tentatively Billy
touched it; his finger came away dirty with grease.
"What's that?" he asked.

"Carburetor, I think," his father said, beaming.

Billy had yearned for a car ever since his father
had taught him to drive, taking him out to back
roads and making him start, stop, and parallel park,
over and over. The lessons had been hard on both
of them. Bill lost patience and once yelled, "Dammit,
are you *trying* to hit every hole in the road?" Nervousness clawed at Billy's stomach, and he grasped
the wheel with sweaty palms; but he passed his driver's test on the first try.

For his seventeenth birthday, Bill gave him the
car: "I hope you like it, son. I always wanted one
when I was your age."

Its black finish was scratched, and the right fender
was dented, and 50,000 miles were on the odometer.
The idling motor coughed and choked as Billy took
it on a run around Beaudale, exalted and still not
believing his luck.

"How was it?" asked his father.

"Can I drive it?" asked Jo-jo.

"It's terrific. Thanks, Dad." Billy faced his father, uncertain whether to hug him or shake hands. Bill stepped back a fraction as Jo-jo repeated, "Can I drive it?"

"Not until you're old enough," his father answered. "It's Billy's car."

"Will you take me for a ride?" asked Evan.

"Honey," his mother said, "now you can do all my shopping for me."

By the next day Billy had lost his euphoria: the engine spluttered fitfully and died at stop signs, a terminal growl surged and faded when he turned the ignition. With a sinking feeling he lifted the hood and stared at the garbled mass of components. He saw the car in months ahead, jerking and gasping into immobility, pushed to the edge of a junk yard, rusting into the ground.

He banged the hood closed so brutally the frame trembled. Savagely he twisted the ignition and pumped the accelerator. The motor wheezed and whined and fouled the air with exhaust. He could not pull into the Esso station and command the mechanics, as his father did, to take a look at something gone wrong. If he were going to salvage the expiring engine, he would have to do it on his own. He slammed the shift into gear and shot down the street toward Kiowa Road and the library.

A terse middle-aged woman led him to the self-help books. He pawed through a shelf of manuals, each as bewildering as the jumble of writhing black wires outside in the parking lot, and finally chose a slim paperback designed for his model and a volume on general maintenance.

Back in his own driveway, the books propped open on the fender, he began to disconnect hoses and clamps, cables and bolts. His touch was gingerly; he was afraid that each twist of a screw would destroy the already decrepit engine, and the whole thing would dissolve under his grasp. Tentatively he removed the fuel line, then fuel filter, peering at each like a pagan priest studying entrails, and compared what he held in his hands to the diagrams on the page. As cautiously as if he were risking an explosion he moved on to the carburetor inlet and fuel pump—tapping, unscrewing, peering, shaking, rubbing, replacing. The rest of the day he groped delicately through the maze.

For a week, every afternoon until the light faded, he hunched over the engine, jiggling wires, squeezing cables, disassembling components, gaining knowledge. As he probed, the labyrinth lost its mystery; each path learned added to Billy's confidence. On the Saturday after he had gotten the car he rose early, spread newspapers on the grass beside the driveway, and raised the hood. He knew, as if he had been reassured by divine vision, that he could cure the stuttering motor.

Bill, in Saturday khakis and faded green flannel shirt, came to peer into the machine. His lips pursed as he squinted at the oily carnage strewn across the newspapers.

"Are you keeping track of this stuff?" he asked.

"Yeah."

"Wouldn't it be better to just do a little bit at a time?"

"No."

"Well," his father said, leaving him, "I hope you know what you're doing, son."

All morning Billy worked, dismantling, polishing, testing, filing points, rubbing away grime, shaking and blowing out grit. At noon his mother called him to lunch, but he said he was not hungry. She brought him a salami sandwich and a glass of milk, and stood by his side while he gulped them down.

"Honey, this is some undertaking."

"Yeah," he said, wiping the milk from his lips with the back of his arm.

"Do you think you can finish it today?" She craned toward the disheveled engine as though she were peeking over a high cliff.

"Yeah, sure."

He began to reassemble the parts. His movements were sure and rapid, and when he turned to the manuals it was only to check impatiently something he already knew. Bert Hardin, beer in hand, walked around the hedge and gazed benignly into the guts of the car.

"Whatcha got here, sport?" he asked. He wore a checkered jacket over his chinos.

"Just tuning it up," said Billy, continuing to work.

Billy's father joined them and Bert said, "Looks like you got a mechanic in the family, Bill." Both men chuckled as they watched Billy tamp a cable into place.

"Yes," said Bill, and his son heard a hint of pride. "I wish I could say he was a chip off the old block, but I got to admit I don't know a damn thing about cars."

"Well, gas makes 'em go, that's all I know."

By four o'clock Billy had almost finished. Though the day was cool and breezy, he had removed his jacket, and his tee shirt and jeans were crusted with grime. Oil smudged his forehead and streaked his arms. His hands were black. Bert left and Harriet joined her husband, a sweater thrown over her shoulders, and they stood side by side at the front of the car, watching him. Evan jumped up on the fender to get a better view.

"Careful, son," said Bill, pulling him back by the shoulder, "don't get in your brother's way."

Jo-jo stood a little apart, an envious sentinel, his nose raised toward the car like a hound pointing game. "What if it won't start?" he asked.

"It'll start," Billy replied, without looking up from the carburetor throat.

"Yeah, but what if it doesn't?"

"Don't bother him," said Bill.

Jo-jo shrugged.

Billy screwed on the air filter top, and looked over the engine, satisfied. He wiped his hands on a grease-sodden rag and slammed the hood closed. The newspapers, greasy and crumpled, now held in place only by rocks and a few filthy tools, rustled in the breeze. He slid nonchalantly into the driver's seat and started the car. The motor purred, then roared as he pressed the accelerator; his family watched as he listened, his ear cocked toward the engine.

"Sounds okay to me," said his father. "How about you?"

Billy listened a few seconds before replying, "Pretty good. There's a little ping there. Might be the ignition. I'll check it out later."

"I sure don't hear anything," said his father. He strained toward the engine in unconscious imitation of his son.

"I can tell better after I take it out for a spin," said Billy.

"You going now?" asked his father.

"Yeah."

"Mind if I come along?"

"Sure."

"Why don't we all go?" said Harriet. To her other sons she asked, "You boys want to take a ride?"

Evan jumped into the car, and Jo-jo, with a why-not grimace, got in beside him. Harriet followed them into the back seat and closed the door. Bill sat in front.

Billy backed out carefully, then gunned the motor and shot up Bradford Street toward Kiowa Road. He pulled to a stop at the light; the motor hummed. He raced it a couple of times, leaning forward with a preoccupied expression.

"How does it sound?" asked his father.

"Pretty good. Okay." He accelerated again. "There might be a little catch in there. I'll check it out."

"Sure sounds okay to me," said Bill, leaning forward.

From the back seat, Jo-jo said, "I don't hear anything."

"What's wrong?" asked Evan. "Didn't you fix it?"

"What are all you boys listening for, anyway?" asked Harriet.

The light changed and Billy turned onto Kiowa Road with a one-handed flourish. He sat hunched over the wheel, his left arm clutching the door through the open window. With both hands he steered through the heavy Saturday phalanx of cars whose back seats brimmed with groceries and children. He turned onto the expressway and speeded up.

"Watch it, son," said Bill. "They patrol this pretty carefully."

"How fast can you make it go?" asked Jo-jo.

"Not too fast, now," said Harriet.

Billy kept his foot on the accelerator, pressing it closer to the floorboard. His father tensed, and the back seat grew quiet as he sped down the inside lane, passing cars with a whoosh.

"I'm cold," said Evan.

The speedometer hit 70, and Billy held it there, leaning forward as if reining in a team of horses.

"I'm cold," Evan whined.

"It's windy back here," yelled Harriet above the rush of air. "Honey, could you roll up your window?"

Billy allowed the needle to fall to 55.

"Well," said Bill. "I hope you don't drive that way all the time."

"Just testing the motor."

"Is that as fast as it'll go?" asked Jo-jo.

"No need to go any faster," said his father. To Billy he added, "I hope you'll be careful, son."

"Sure." He felt excited and powerful, beyond criticism.

"We're coming to the turn-off," said his father. "You ought to put your signal on."

Indifferently Billy flipped the signal up and edged to the right.

"You're going too fast, son."

"I'm okay," said Billy. "Do we need anything before we go home?" He looked at his mother in the rear view mirror.

"Nothing," said Harriet. "Everything's ready for supper."

They rode through the towns that flowed into each other along Kiowa Road, past the Friendly Restaurant and Drive In, the Esso station, the Bumberden Nursery, and Perryville Shopping Mall.

Just before Billy turned into Bradford Street, a red Thunderbird coming from the other direction honked twice sharply. The driver, Billy's age, with long black hair and aviator sunglasses, sat with his left arm hooked over his open window; he raised his thumb and fist in salute.

"Friend of yours?" asked Bill.

"Sort of."

"He's that guy from California," said Jo-jo, impressed.

"He looks like a nice boy," said Harriet.

"Yeah, he's okay." He turned into Bradford Street and their driveway.

"Well, son," said Bill solemnly, "Congratulations. I'll be honest with you—I was frankly a little worried this morning when I saw you taking this thing apart."

"Thanks," Billy mumbled. He raced the engine a couple of times before cutting off the ignition. "It still needs some work."

Billy lavished attention on the car. He accumulated tools—a torque wrench, a spark-plug feeler gauge, an ignition file—that permitted more sophisticated adjustments. He rewired the motor, drained the transmission fluid, and changed the brake-sleeves. Cherishing the machine, he responded to its slightest gasp, its faintest hesitation.

It was more than locomotion; the car allowed him to roar away from the crowd at school rather than be abandoned by it.

Billy had been certain that high school would be different from grade school; he was optimistic as he entered the huge building. He convinced himself that he despised the enclave of basketball players, brains, cheerleaders, quarterbacks and running ends who constituted the different spheres of the high school aristocracy. He called himself a loner, yet he always had a few companions: others who for one reason or another—stuttering or obesity or acne—felt too flawed to vie for space in the golden circles. But he knew that they, like him, could find no one else to spare them the shame of being alone.

His father never gauged the depth of his unpopularity. Bill had got him into the Little League and, for his twelfth birthday, had given him a set of boxing gloves, telling him to mix it up with his buddies. Billy hid the gloves in his locker at school.

Once Billy was in high school his father had fewer opportunities to goad him into social or athletic arenas. Whenever he could, however, Bill met his son's friends.

"That new buddy of yours, Everett, seems like a nice guy. What's his dad do?"

"I dunno. Something with chemicals, I think."

"I haven't seen him around before."

"They just moved here a few months ago."

"He's a big boy. Does he play football?"

"No. Maybe a little."

"They're missing a good chance if they don't get him on the team. It'd be good for him, too. He could toughen up a little—get rid of the softness there. He's a little overweight."

"Yeah."

"But bright, I bet."

"Yeah, he's okay."

Bill's comments were usually hopeful and encouraging. When, inevitably, the buddy faded from view—was sent to a private school, or, in one case, was hospitalized after a breakdown—he hailed the appearance of a new buddy. Sometimes, though, he balked. "That kid I saw you with this afternoon—wasn't that Bob Raymond's kid?"

"I dunno. His name's Joe Raymond, so maybe."

"Well, son, the Raymonds really aren't the sort of people you want to get mixed up with."

"Joe's okay."

"That may be, but his father's a deadbeat and a drunk and is probably going to lose their home for nonpayment . . . and his mother's nothing to write home about either."

"I never met his mother or father."

"You know, son, family background's important. Not everyone's as lucky as you and your brothers—to have the kind of family life you have. . . ."

"Yeah."

"It's important to choose your buddies carefully. Now, I'm not snobbish, God knows, but I just don't want to see you fall into the wrong crowd. Jerry Hardin seems to run with a pretty good bunch of guys. . . ."

"He's on the football team," said Billy sullenly. "He runs around with that gang. Besides, Grace and Bert drink."

Bill compressed his lips. "They're not drunkards. And they keep up their house payments. There's a big difference between Bert Hardin and Bob Raymond. Take my word for it. Someday you'll understand."

Billy shrugged, his face set stubbornly. Within weeks, however, the Raymonds had lost their house and left Beaudale.

There were a few figures in high school that Billy envied and admired. One of these appeared during his junior year. Norton Hall, a transfer student from California, rode onto the parking lot in a red Thunderbird at mid-term, black hair to his shoulders, aviator glasses, a swagger that grew from insolence rather than fear, and a pronounced indifference toward students and teachers. From the corner of his eye Billy watched the newcomer, waiting sourly to see who would take him in: Would he go out for football? He had the build. Or basketball? Maybe band? As weeks lengthened to months Norton kept alone. He was impervious to blandishments; his isolation was self-imposed, not like Billy's, which had been spawned by intimidation.

Bits and pieces of the new boy's past bobbed up on the gossipy current swirling through the school: He was a surfer and a mountain climber; he hated the East where he had been forced to come because his father had gained custody of him; he was only biding time until he could get back West where he was happy; he truly wanted nothing to do with anything or anybody at Beaudale High. Norton made no compromises, cultivated no ersatz friends. One day in the cafeteria he was caught short at the cash register; Billy stood behind him and with careful disinterest offered to loan him fifty cents.

"Thanks, man," Norton said, "I'll get it back to you this afternoon."

"No sweat, man," Billy replied, matching his tone.

From then on Norton nodded as they crossed in the halls.

The Saturday afternoon that Norton passed Billy in his Thunderbird and gave a thumbs-up signal marked a new stage in their rapport; they began to exchange whole sentences, mostly about their cars. Norton knew a lot about his engine, and had accumulated many professional tools—lavished on him by a father trying to compensate for the lack of surf and mountains.

"Man, you need any of this shit, just take it," said Norton with an indifferent shrug toward the rack of gleaming tools.

"That's great, man," Billy replied, uneasy in the big, spotless garage with its built-in cabinets for gardening tools and lawn furniture. The concrete floor appeared to have been waxed.

"Keep 'em as long as you need 'em."

"Great. Say, maybe you wanna take in a movie
. . . say, this weekend. . . ."

Before he could finish the sentence, Billy saw a
glaze cover Norton's eyes.

"Can't, man. Another time."

Billy did not have the courage to press for more.
Limited as it was, the friendship nurtured the self-
confidence the car had sown.

The car had also led him to the Sheffields.

Once he had coaxed the Cobra into shape he began
to roam up and down Kiowa Road, exploring the
inlets and caverns of neighboring towns: pizza par-
lors, movie houses, pinball arcades—all were exciting
when he happened onto them in his own car, usually
with two or three of the guys. He was a senior in
high school, and soon would be a college man. He
was rarely afraid any more. He walked with new
authority—shoulders back, eyes fixed straight ahead,
mouth set. His friends, the guys, were still drawn
from the same marshy fringes. He had withdrawn
so completely from the center of the high school
establishment he was hardly noticed.

Billy still gazed with dour longing at those students
who seemed to glow with reflected approval—Jerry
Hardin was one—but he was consoled by the certainty he would leave them all behind in less than
a year. He would be starting over; college would
complete the liberation the car had begun.

One evening he had driven with three of the guys
to Perryville to watch a basketball game. They took

seats on the Perryville side of the bleachers, under exposed steel rafters and a vaulted ceiling that amplified the howl of the crowd and the claps and chants of short-skirted cheerleaders. ("Gimme a P!" Clap clap. "Gimme an E!" Clap clap. . . .) Billy slouched, his elbows on his knees, to show that he was not impressed by anything he saw or was likely to see. As players dodged, danced, and rushed from one end of the gymnasium to the other, he remained aloof while those around him leaped and screamed.

The girl next to him was as restrained as he; with a sideways glance he noticed her passivity—hands on blue-jeaned lap, blue and white sneakered feet crossed at the ankles. She smelled sweet and was thin. When he dared to glance at her directly he found her profile as unemotional as the rest of her. Her skin was delicately tinted around the cheeks and her fine chestnut hair, softly curling to her shoulders, shone clean. Her nose was slightly turned up, as were the corners of her lips. He wanted her to notice him.

The ball slipped through the basket, leaving a trembling net and setting off more screaming in the stands. Beside him the girl looked down at her hands, then with her index finger idly scratched her knee. Billy dared another direct glance; she seemed resigned, like someone waiting in a doctor's office.

He cleared his throat. "Is that your team?" he asked.

She looked at him, startled. "Which one?" Her brown eyes widened with confusion; her voice was tiny, and there were braces on her teeth. She was younger than he.

"The one that just made the basket," he said, with more assurance.

She looked at the court quickly. "I don't . . . I wasn't paying much attention . . . I really don't know much about it," she said, apologetic. She blushed. Two girls with her appraised Billy; they were animated and the one nearest was stridently vocal about the game. The shy girl said something to her; she replied while darting quick glances at Billy.

"Yes," the chestnut-haired girl said to him then, "that was our team. Perryville . . ."

"You go to Perryville?" Billy asked.

"Yes."

"I go to Beaudale. I'm Billy Johnson."

"How do you do." She smiled timidly. Then, blushing again, she added, "I'm Wilma Sheffield."

He wondered whether they should shake hands, but she kept hers on her lap. "I don't care much for basketball, either," he said. To his own ears he sounded stuffy. "I mean, I don't play it much."

"Me, neither."

Beside her the loud girl screeched "Come on Jimmy!" as she jumped up and down theatrically.

Wilma quietly explained, "Her brother's on the team. That's him." She pointed.

"Is that why you came?"

"She's my friend," said Wilma. She glanced at him, less shy. "Why did you?"

"Something to do," he said with a shrug. "Me and some guys just drove over."

"Oh."

He added, "I just decided to drive here in my car." Then he felt like a clumsy braggart. "No big deal."

She nodded gravely.

"Do you need a ride home?" he asked.

Her lips parted in surprise before she looked away, embarrassed. "My mother's picking us up," she said.

He felt bold, intoxicated with self-confidence. "Well, maybe another time? I mean, maybe I could come by and go to a movie or something?"

She smiled, demure, but not coquettish. "Yes," she said. Her companions and his were watching them surreptitiously. One of his gave him a jab in the ribs and another hissed something that cracked them up. Wilma's friend whispered in her ear; she shook her head no.

Billy and Wilma's conversation for the rest of the game was laconic and cautious: she did not like cokes; he never cared much for cats; they both liked Bruce Springsteen. At the end of the game Wilma and Billy filed out of the gymnasium together, followed by their friends, two diplomatic retinues uncertain of protocol. In the parking lot Billy learned Wilma's phone number, and repeated it several times. They had just said goodby when a tall, thin woman in pants and a bulky Mexican sweater came striding toward them.

"Wilma," she called. "Over here." She smiled at Billy. "Hi," she said, extending her hand. "I'm Betty Sheffield, Wilma's mother."

Billy was shaking her hand before thinking.

"How was the game?" asked Betty.

"Fine," they both said, then looked at each other and giggled.

"Who won?"

"We did," said Wilma.

"Well," said Betty, "I guess we better gather up everyone and get on home." She asked Billy, "You have a ride?" Her voice was nasal and eager.

"I have my own car," he said.

"Billy's from Beaudale," Wilma told her mother.

"You want to come by for some hot chocolate?" She looked over Wilma's head and asked, "You girls want to come by for some hot chocolate?" Before giving them a chance to answer she returned to Billy. "You're certainly welcome, and your friends, too."

"Thanks," he said, "but I guess we better be getting back."

"Well, it sure was nice meeting you," Betty said, extending her hand again. "Be sure and come by and see us, now."

He and Wilma waved as she and her mother left, followed by her two friends.

"Oh, boy," said one of the guys, "what a make-out artist."

"Shut up," Billy said fiercely.

He had phoned two days later and made a date. At first he was reserved and austere. He felt he was on probation. *"Why* did I say *that?"* he would groan to himself, alone in his car, driving back to Beaudale. He stood when Wilma's mother or father came into the room and called them "sir" and "ma'am," and blushed a lot. Alone with Wilma he was considerate and protective. They kissed on the second date, and he tentatively touched her ribcage just below her small breasts, but when she stiffened he did not go any further.

After a few weeks his rigidity dissolved in Betty's relentless and shrewd good cheer. "Do you think," she said one day, "that your tongue would fall out if you called me 'Betty' instead of 'Mrs. Sheffield'? Every time you talk to me I begin to be afraid I'm my mother-in-law." She had laughed and he had blushed, but he had started calling her Betty.

Their house was unlike any he had ever been in. On the outside it was a series of redwood rectangles with diamond shaped windows that sat jauntily on a corner lot and declared its difference from the surrounding Cape Cod and colonial styles. It had been designed by an architect friend of Betty's. Inside, the living and dining rooms faced onto an interior open court in which a tiny Japanese garden displayed one convoluted grey rock, a few stalks of bamboo, and some chrysanthemum and azalea plants dotting a patch of pristine white pebbles. In the den was a television set that had a screen measured in feet rather than inches, but no one looked at it very much. "It's okay for news, I guess," said Betty, "and maybe a few other things, but honestly, the junk they peddle. . . ." Scattered on end tables were copies of *Rolling Stone, Ms.,* and *Mother Jones.*

Billy watched covertly to see if the Sheffields used their knives or forks differently from other people, but if anything they seemed more relaxed around the dinner table than his own family. He was shocked once to see Betty casually pluck a lettuce leaf out of the salad bowl with her fingers and pop it into her mouth.

After a while he relaxed more, though he never really let his guard down when with the whole family. He was at ease with Wilma, who was always glad to see him, but it was Betty who made him feel respected and grownup.

Freely she talked about her years as a missionary in Taiwan along with her first husband (she had married in college back in Texas), and freely she talked about her divorce. She mentioned in passing that she and her present husband, Gary, had lived together for a couple of years before marrying; both had marched in Selma, and Betty had been one of the first women in New York to work in an abortion counseling clinic.

"I never thought," Betty said one time, "I'd ever end up in New Jersey." She laughed. "All my life I wanted to live in New York City—and I did for just two years. And then we came out here. We might as well have moved to South Dakota." She shrugged with a wry smile. "Oh, well, we did it for the girls. Do you think you're better off here than you would be in New York?" she asked Wilma, teasing.

"New York is scary," her daughter replied.

Billy was fascinated by the range of Betty's causes: women's rights and the right to abortion; legalization of marijuana (though she forbade her daughters to use it and Billy never admitted to her that he smoked); the sale of baby formula to third-world countries; the plight of migrant workers in California. Her concern for the underdog—any underdog, any-where—was boundless and passionate.

Betty was not really pretty, but she was so vivacious she seemed to be. It was a shock the day Billy realized that she was probably the same age as his mother.

"Billy! You old sweetheart!" she yelled once from the front door as he was getting out of his car. "You are the only bright spot in my day." She was wearing a pink tank top with jeans, and she put her bare scented arms around his shoulders and hugged him as he blushed.

She was curious about him, but it was not easy for him to talk. In her sleek living room his concerns seemed shabby or petty or out of place. But it was

she who first learned about his decision to attend
school in the South, even before his father knew.

"They say it's one of the best of its kind," he said
shyly, watching for her approval.

"I've heard a little about it," she replied carefully.
"I wouldn't have thought a military school was your
best bet. . . ."

"It's rough, you mean? I can handle that."

She laughed, teasing. "I'm sure you can. It's just
that a *military* school . . . well, I don't know. . . ."

"It's better than going around here," he said de-
fensively.

"Getting away is always a good idea, I suppose."

"It isn't as though I was accepted by one of the
ivy league schools, or something like that. . . ."

"You didn't try, Billy."

"My grades weren't that good. My counselor at
school said this was a good choice, all things consid-
ered." He sulked, disappointed at her reaction.

She squeezed his arm. "Listen, kiddo, if you want
to go to that school, that's fine with me."

Wilma did not appear to mind that her mother
and Billy had become such good friends. She seemed
so placid that even her few eruptions met at most
an exasperated sigh from her mother.

Wilma and Billy did not talk about much. After
the first few dates, when Billy had proved that he
could kiss her, they settled into a companionable,
hand-holding friendship. When he was teased by the
guys about knocking off a piece, he said nothing one

way or the other. After he became established at
the Sheffields, he saw less of the guys.

The night before Billy left to go South, Betty
served a farewell dinner by candlelight. She wore a
crimson caftan and long golden earrings that tinkled
when she moved, and she insisted her daughters and
husband dress up also. The August night was sticky
and close, but the dining room, with its view of the
Japanese garden, was cool and softly glowing as the
Sheffields raised their glasses for Betty's toast: "Here's
to Billy and his bright, *bright* future!"

He had not blushed nor stammered, but had risen
and said, simply, "Here's to all of you," as he darted
a quick look at Betty, who sat smiling at her end of
the table. Before he and Wilma left for the drive-
in, Betty kissed his cheek and hugged him and said,
"Now I want you to let us know *everything* that
happens to you down there, you hear?" His eyes had
stung and for a horrified instant he thought he might
cry, but he recovered and said gruffly, "I sure will,
Betty. And thanks a lot." He had turned abruptly
and led Wilma to the car.

He had written, and Wilma had answered on pastel
blue, scented paper, with fat, well-formed characters
arabesquing across a page or two, and symmetrical
little "x"'s under her signature. His letters were at
first dutifully descriptive—the town, the campus, the
weather—but as he mired deeper into despair they
degenerated into truncated greetings, as terse as
telegrams. As he flew home, it was Betty he explained

everything to in his imagination. Yet no matter how carefully he rehearsed the story, he could not make himself the hero of it. His shame contaminated the Sheffields; he decided he would stay away from Perryville until he could mold events into a shape more flattering to him. But his need was too strong. Only a few hours after he arrived, he called.

Now, on Friday evening, lights glowed from the diamond windows as he pulled up to the curb in front of the redwood rectangles. On the front door someone, Betty, probably, had tied a sheaf of dried stained corn in celebration of Thanksgiving. He turned off the motor and stepped from the car into suburban silence. The door swung open and Betty whooped, "Billy! I knew it had to be you! I've made us some coffee!"

She hugged him as his arms hung awkwardly at his sides. "My goodness, but you've gotten even thinner and *taller*. What are they feeding you down there?" She glanced at his forehead and quickly looked away, as, laughing, she took his hand and led him toward the kitchen. "Gary and the girls are picking up some stuff for the weekend so we've got time to have a little talk. Now then," she said as she positioned him in front of a kitchen chair and gently shoved his chest until he sat, "I want you to talk to me *fast* and tell me everything that has happened while I've got you to myself. You want some coffee?"

She was wearing blue jeans with a bulky white sweater that fell to her hips. Her hair was shorter than it had been in August, but everything else was unchanged: the brown eyes were still wide with flattering attention, and her expressions were a kaleidoscope of delight as she watched him.

"Okay, now talk," she said, pulling her chair up to the table and putting her chin on her palm as she leaned toward him. "What do you think of it?"

"The school? It's okay." He left his cup on the table.

"Umm. Is that all?"

He shrugged, still not looking at her. "Well, you know, it's like, I haven't been there for very long."

"But you like it?"

"Well. . . ."

"You don't, do you?"

"Well, not really. . . ."

"Why not?"

"Oh, it's just that the other . . . I don't know."

"What are the other kids like?"

"Oh, you know, they're okay, I guess, but. . . ."

"But what, Billy?" She put her hand on his arm and squeezed gently. "What's wrong?"

He stared mutely at the table between them for a long moment before shaking his head slowly. "I just don't fit in."

She was silent, waiting.

"I tried to, you know, get along, but. . . ." Tears coursed down his nose and dropped on the walnut table near his coffee cup. They both stared at the splotches staining the polished wood, as others fell beside them. Then, as though he had broken through an ice hole after swimming frantically underwater, he gulped in a great lungful of air and sobbed. His face contorted with the effort, but he could not staunch the flow. Both were stunned by the violence of the outburst. He cried noisily, tears streaming from his eyes, and mucus dribbling from his nose, and in spite of all his will power and shame, he could not stop. He sat, head bowed over the table.

Betty pulled him to her. She cradled his head against her breasts and caressed him while crooning, over and over, "Oh, Billy, Billy, Billy . . . there, there . . . it's going to be all right. . . ."

Still he could not stop. He wiped his nose on his sleeve, ashamed of the gob deposited there, but unable to hide it. He was unable, it seemed, to hide anything. He felt open, vulnerable, disgusting—and still he cried.

"There, there, there," Betty chanted softly into his ear, kissing his forehead, smoothing his hair. "There, there, there . . . you'll feel better after it's all out. . . ."

Finally he subsided, drained, as gasping, spasmodic sobs erupted like jetsam bobbing to the surface after a shipwreck.

Betty fetched Kleenex and wiped his nose. He turned his head away, his swollen red eyes despondent.

"Now, now," said Betty softly, "let's get to the bottom of this."

"I'm sorry."

"Billy, you've got nothing to be sorry about. Look at me, Billy. You hear what I'm saying?"

He nodded.

"Now, what's wrong?"

"I'm not a sissy."

"I know that. Good God, I know that. Is that what it is? Did they—those people down there—did they make fun of you?"

"I . . . don't fit in."

She touched the bruise on his forehead. "Did they do that to you?"

He shied from her hand.

"How did this happen?"

He shook his head. "I don't want to go back."

"Well, you don't have to. For Christ's sake, if you feel this strongly about it, whatever makes you think you have to go back? What do your folks say?"

"They say I'll get used to it."

"They *what!*"

"I didn't tell them, I mean, they didn't . . . ." He flung his hands out helplessly.

"You've told them you don't like the place?"

He nodded.

"Then surely they won't send you back?"

"I guess I've got to go."

"Why?"

"Because . . . I don't want to let them down."

"Who?"

"My family . . . my dad. . . ."

"That's silly! They don't want to make a martyr of you. Who said you'd be letting them down? Is that what they told you?"

He shook his head.

"Maybe you haven't explained to them? I mean, told them exactly how much you hate it?"

"Yes, I did."

"Well . . . ?"

"He . . . Dad . . . says I can't run away every time something bad happens, that I've got to be responsible."

"Oh, for Christ's sake!"

Billy looked at her, confused.

"Now, you listen. You do *not* have to go back to that place. If your father is dumb enough to try to send you back you just get in that car of yours and drive away. You're eighteen years old, Billy! Go to New York City, and get some kind of job until they come to their senses. I'll give you money if you need it. You don't even have to swim the Hudson. You can just drive across that bridge and be on your own." She paced the kitchen. Billy watched her with surprised, guilty eyes. He felt he had betrayed his father.

"You don't understand . . ." he began weakly.

Fiercely she turned on him. "I understand that you are one miserable young man. I understand that.

And there is no reason for it. That damned school! I thought it was a mistake when I first heard about it."

"It's not a bad school," he muttered.

"It's not for *you*, Billy." She stopped pacing as suddenly as she had begun, and sat down next to him. "Do you want me to talk to your father?" she asked.

He was appalled. "No. No, I don't want . . . I don't know. . . ."

"Then I want *you* to talk to him, you hear? I want you to tell him that you are wretched in that place and that you must not go back. When were you supposed to leave?"

"Sunday night."

"Promise me that you'll have this out with him. Will you promise me that?" She held both his hands and leaned forward until her face was only inches from his.

"Yes," he said.

"I'm going to call you Sunday afternoon." She took his face between her hands and looked at him an instant before saying, "Billy, you are too nice a person to have to go through crap like this."

He could see the minute flecks of green in her iris. Her mouth was slightly open, showing even teeth, and the sweetness of her breath mingled with the delicate scent of her hair, the clean odor of her cool hands. His own mouth was open, and he breathed shallow, his chest immobilized in anticipation of an event he could not imagine. His face was flushed; he still felt the softness of her breasts on his cheeks. Involuntarily he leaned even closer, and saw her eyes widen with surprise, or understanding or decision— he could not tell.

A car door slammed, and they both tensed. Betty patted his cheek and laughed quickly. "Go wash your face."

He stood immediately. "You won't say anything about . . . ." His hand swept vaguely above the table as though he were clearing away his tears and words, like the messy remains of a meal.

"This is between us," said Betty, rising and hugging him. "I'm on your side."

Over the bathroom sink he squinted at his face as he splashed handful after handful of cold water on it. After he had washed he remained at the mirror, composing his features into a series of expressions— calm, disdainful, nonchalant, arrogant—but was unable to make any stick. Embarrassment kept flooding his eyes. Finally he shook his head in frustration, and left the bathroom.

Gary Sheffield greeted him with familiar good humor. "Well, boy, we thought you might have fallen in. Good to see you, Billy." He extended his hand, and Billy shook it. "So, how's it going down there? You learn the Rebel yell, yet?"

"No."

"Just as well." Gary was lean and handsome, with black hair greying at the temples, and kindly eyes behind aviator glasses. He wore jeans, sweater, and sneakers, and from the back might have been taken for someone much younger.

"Hi," said Wilma shyly. Her sister, Alice, smiled coolly to show she was no more impressed now than before.

"Hi. Good to see you."

"What are you kids—excuse me, you young *people*—planning to do?" Betty asked gaily. "Nothing that's going to keep you out very late, I hope?" Her tone was ironic, as she smoothed Wilma's hair away from her forehead.

Billy did not look at her directly as he answered, "I thought we might go to a movie, if that's okay."

"Sure," said Wilma.

"That sounds like a nice evening," said Betty. "Have a good time." She took Billy's hand, forcing him to face her. "It's great to have you back home, Billy."

"Thanks."

She held his eyes for an instant, then smiled and squeezed his hand. "Remember now, I want to talk to you again soon," she said. "You promise?"

He dropped his eyes. "Sure," he mumbled. Then he pulled away and led Wilma out the front door.

They ended up just driving around, stopping for sodas, then driving some more.

"Are you glad to be back?" Wilma asked.

"Yeah."

"I guess you won't be back again until just before Christmas."

"Yeah."

" 'Yeah,' " she mimicked him.

He smiled.

"You like it down there?" She snuggled closer and took his hand.

"Yeah. I mean, it's okay."

"I'd like to see it sometime."

He was silent.

"Not for a while, but maybe next year. . . . Will you send me a picture in your uniform?"

Her admiration touched off both pride and self-revulsion. "Maybe."

He felt her withdraw, hurt by his brusqueness.

"Well, don't bother if it's too much trouble." She edged to her side of the car.

He drove in a silence that grew more uncomfortable. Wilma looked out her window, her hands on her lap.

"I guess we ought to, maybe, make an early night of it," he said over the hum of the motor.

"Okay by me." She continued staring out the window.

"I'm not very . . . I'm just not with it tonight."

"That's okay."

"Maybe I can call tomorrow?"

"If you want to."

As he pulled up in front of the redwood rectangles, the warm light from the diamond windows beckoned invitingly. Wilma politely asked, "Do you want to come in for a little while?"

He thought of Betty at the kitchen table. "I guess not," he said. "Not tonight. I'm sorry I was, you know, such bad company."

"That's okay." She smiled quickly, with hurt eyes, and got out of the car. "Good night."

He drove away before she reached the front door.

Chapter Seven

Everything should have worked out differently.

In August the Johnsons pulled out of the driveway on the first leg of their trip south to put their oldest son in college. Glittering on Billy's ego like a medal was his acceptance into the military academy.

He had always known he would go to college. His father had predicted reproachfully, "You're going to have the kind of chance I never had," or threateningly, "They won't put up with grades like that in a university," or sentimentally, "You'll make buddies in college that'll be with you all the rest of your life."

Billy's future assumed more shape in his junior year, when all around him the talk was of who was trying for what college. Billy could not say exactly when going to West Point first seized his imagination, but the desire grew, fed by his yearning to become one of those cadets with square shoulders, a stiff back, and a strong jaw. In his mind's eye, he resembled a recruiting poster.

His counselor was discouraging. "That's a tough nut to crack—a hard row to hoe, you know what I mean? Many are called but few are chosen." He was a mild man in his late twenties, with sparse blond hair and silver-rimmed glasses. "You've got to get, you know, recommendations from senators and people like that, and since it's a scholarship you have to rank pretty high in your class. And, you know, those schools are *tough*—I mean, they really put a guy through the ropes. . . ."

"That's where I want to go," said Billy.

The man looked annoyed and made a note. "Well, we'll get things rolling. But you better apply to a couple of other places too, just to be safe. Huh?"

"Yes, sir."

"If you really want military schools," the counselor continued, taking a blue book from the shelf behind him, "we can consider some of these. . . ." He leafed through the pages. Billy wanted only West Point, but he went along with the suggestion, and applied to several other schools.

His father encouraged him. "By golly," Bill said, "the army's the one career that's recession proof. You go through West Point and you can write your own ticket." He became active in the local Republican club in order to get closer to their congressman, whose endorsement he courted and won. "Contacts," he told Billy, "are what get you ahead in this world. This is a great country, but you got to know the right people to make it work for you."

But friends in high places could not improve Billy's eyesight. The letter of rejection did not mention his SAT score or other qualifications, but stated simply that the candidate could not pass the Academy's physical requirements. Billy was ashamed to show it to his father.

Bill read rapidly, lips tightened. "Dammit, that's what glasses are for. You see just fine with them, don't you?"

"Yeah."

"Well, if worse comes to worse, there's always Fairleigh Dickinson."

The southern military school accepted Billy, and sent him a catalogue and a brochure across which was printed, "Where manhood meets mastery." Pictured under the slogan were ranks of crisply uniformed young men, all handsome, all looking like Billy looked to himself in daydreams.

Tentatively he offered it to his father, who took it with a shrug, leafed through it, then turned down the corners of his mouth while raising his eyebrows above the thick black frames of his glasses. "The price is right," Bill said.

There were pictures of the campus—crenellated towers, serene facades, and huge old oaks—and happy, healthy cadets vigorously pursuing higher education. The college was founded before the Civil

War, in which it played a germinal and glorious part, and had spawned great men. A degree conferred a commission in the United States Army.

Within days both father and son were enthusiastic. "That's the kind of school that counts," Bill said to Bert Hardin. "A degree from there means something."

Bert nodded affably. "Yep. It's the real thing." His voice rumbled from an exudate of tobacco and alcohol.

"I tell you, this business of schools is no laughing matter."

"No, sir. Not like when I was a kid. I doubt I could even get into one today."

"What about Jerry . . ." Bill suggested delicately.

"Well, all I can say is thank God for football. Looks like he might have a scholarship to Penn State."

"Now that's terrific," said Bill. "Isn't that something."

Bert turned to Billy. "So, hotshot, you gonna be a military man?"

"Yeah."

"Well, your work's cut out for you," and he launched into a denunciation of selling out in Vietnam.

Billy strutted through the halls of Beaudale High during his last months, nodding only to Norton and a few others: it was easy to float above the crowd when you knew you would be leaving it behind.

As he slipped under the wheel of his mother's station wagon the sultry August morning of departure, he felt like a young prince on whom the hopes of a kingdom had been hung. His clothes had been tagged, his eyes and teeth checked, his few farewells made. The baggage had been packed the night before and the car tuned and waxed.

Billy drove steadily, his arm propped on the open window, his father beside him, his mother and brothers in the back seat. They rolled along Interstate 95 going south, through Delaware, Maryland, and Virginia, learning only by signs when they moved from one state to another. Jo-jo and Evan bickered, and Bill dozed, and Harriet would look up from her paperback from time to time at the concrete sameness and comment on the nice scenery. Billy was in charge.

His father's plan was to take a leisurely two-day trip and stop somewhere in the afternoon, but as the day wore on Bill became impatient to get there. "Maybe we should drive straight on through—what do you think?"

"Whatever you say, honey," Harriet replied unhappily.

"I'm tired," said Evan.

"You haven't done anything but sit there," said Jo-jo.

"I don't care, I'm tired."

"We'll be there in a little while," said Harriet automatically.

"It might not be a bad idea just to go ahead and get the trip over with," said Bill.

"I thought we were going to stay at one of those motels with a swimming pool," said Jo-jo.

No one answered.

"Why can't we stop at one of those motels with a swimming pool," Jo-jo said aggressively. "I don't see why we have to make it in one day."

"We don't *have* to," said Bill shortly. "It just might be better to drive straight through."

"Better for who?" asked Jo-jo.

Bill compressed his lips. After a moment he asked Billy, "Are you tired, son?"

"No. I'm fine." Billy did not care whether they stopped or drove all night. He was as indefatigable as the car, a part of the engine that hummed so steadily.

"I'm tired," Evan whined.

"Well," said Bill, "maybe we ought to consider stopping somewhere for the night."

"I thought that's what we were going to do all along," said Jo-jo, disgusted.

Harriet put her hand on his knee and shook her head. Bill looked straight ahead, controlling his anger.

Later, Bill said, "Let's keep an eye out for a motel." They had crossed into North Carolina.

"One with a swimming pool," said Jo-jo.

"I'm hungry," said Evan.

"If we pass a service station that looks clean, I'd like to stop," said Harriet.

"Me too," said Jo-jo.

"Can you hold it a little longer?" asked Bill, turning to Harriet. "For another half hour or so?"

"I guess." She opened her book abruptly and became ostentatiously absorbed in it.

Following Bill's direction, Billy turned off the Interstate at Raleigh, and drove onto a narrower road bristling with advertisements for motels. The family shook itself out of its grumpy lethargy and sat up. Evan leaned over his father's shoulder, his arms folded on the back of the seat. Harriet closed her book and Jo-jo studied the road signs.

They pulled into a motel that Harriet said looked nice. A two-story tan stucco building with a red roof formed a large U, and in the center was a small irregularly shaped pool that glistened emptily in the late afternoon sun.

Billy stretched, arching his back and extending his arms over his head. He was as content as he could ever remember being.

"Can we go swimming, daddy?" asked Evan after they had checked in.

"I guess. I don't see why not." Turning to Harriet, he smiled. "Well, mother, how're you travelling?"

"Just fine," said Harriet, walking a little unsteadily.

The boys changed into their bathing suits and ran to the pool. From the doorway of his room Bill called, "Don't dive! It doesn't look deep enough for diving!"

But Jo-jo dove anyway, and surfaced to swim the short distance to the end in a few seconds, then back again. "It's *cold,*" he said and swam again, splashing water onto the poolside. Billy and Evan jumped in and Harriet and Bill came and watched them. "Aren't you going to swim, daddy?" called Evan.

"No, your mother and I are lifeguards," said Bill. His arm was around Harriet as she nestled into his shoulder, and they watched their family.

They showered and changed. Bill wore tan slacks and a short-sleeved blue sports shirt; Harriet put on a light rust cotton dress and white beads with matching earrings. The boys wore clean jeans and tee shirts. Bill drove the mile to the restaurant recommended by the desk clerk. It had a carpet and soft lights with red shades, and waitresses in yellow starched uniforms. The Johnsons' waitress, a small wiry woman with a determined sprightliness, greeted them with a big smile and a drawled welcome that Jo-jo imitated as soon as she had left the table. Then Evan imitated Jo-jo, and Bill had to reprimand them both: "Remember we're guests here. Behave as though you were in someone's home. You wouldn't make fun of your hostess in her home, would you?"

"If she talked like that, I would," said Jo-jo.

"Tch tch," said Harriet. "She seems like a very nice lady."

Billy, invested with an authority that grew stronger
the further he travelled from home, said, "You guys
knock it off."

The waitress returned and asked, "Y'all want a
drink before dinner?"

Bill thoughtfully said, "Well, now, mother, what
do you say? Let's have a little something?"

"Okay," said Harriet blithely. "I think I'd like a
manhattan."

"A manhattan," repeated the waitress.

"A martini for me. Very dry," said Bill.

"For me, too," said Jo-jo, causing the waitress to
smile and say, "You're gonna have to wait a little
while for yours, honey."

The drinks came and Bill toasted Harriet, then
Billy. Bill and Harriet sipped slowly, and both pronounced their drinks very good. "In fact," said Bill,
leaning back against the booth, "I think I could
stand another one. How about you, mother?"

"Oh," said Harriet, smiling and flushed, "I don't
know. I suppose so."

They all grew more animated with the second
round of cocktails as though the boys as well as their
parents were drinking them. Harriet's eyes sparkled
and her color heightened, and Bill laughed even at
Jo-jo's wisecracks. Everyone had a side order of grits.

"Better get used to them, son," said Bill, gingerly
tasting them at the end of his tongue.

"They're a little like potatoes," said Harriet.

"They're like nothing at all," said Jo-jo, salting his.

"Well," said Harriet, "I suppose the people around here like them."

They had dessert, and when the waitress brought the check she asked, "You folks travelling through, or are you gonna stay for a while?"

"No," said Bill, "we're on our way to put our boy here in college. Gonna smarten him up."

They laughed. "You sure do have a fine family," said the waitress. She smiled and Bill thanked her as the rest modestly looked at the table.

On the way back to the car, Bill and Harriet held hands as they followed their boys.

"Why don't you drive us back, son," said Bill to Billy. "Your mother and I are going to ride in the back seat."

"Oh, Bill," giggled Harriet. Embarrassed, she said to her sons, "Isn't he awful?"

Billy drove the mile past motels and coffee shops and pulled into a parking space near their rooms.

"Well," said Bill, "we've got a long day tomorrow, so you boys don't stay up too late. You gonna watch TV?"

"Yeah," said Billy.

"Your mother and I are going to turn in. Us old folks need our rest." He smiled at Harriet.

They said goodnight and as soon as Evan was out of earshot Jo-jo said to Billy, "They're gonna fuck."

The boys' beige room had two single beds and a cot, a TV, telephone, bedside lamps, and two chairs. Jo-jo clicked the TV from station to station, then looked at Billy meaningfully and declared there wasn't much he wanted to see, and maybe he'd take a little walk. Evan uncritically settled in to watch an old movie. The two older boys went out by the pool, empty under floodlights, then walked further to shadows behind the motel and Jo-jo pulled a skinny, frazzled joint out of his hip pocket.

"How long you been carrying this around?" Billy asked.

"It's okay." Jo-jo lighted it and sucked in, containing smoke while offering it to Billy.

Billy inhaled and passed it back, and they both looked reflectively from the darkness out toward the lighted highway where cars streaked past. The silence grew self-conscious, and Jo-jo broke it.

"You excited?"

"About school? Sort of."

"Maybe I'll go there too. I mean, when it's time for me to go to college." In the dark Jo-jo sounded shy, as though he were angling for an invitation.

"Sure, why not."

"You gonna write letters?"

"Sure."

They watched cars in the distance and listened to the faint hum of their motors. Billy cleared his throat and said, "You know, I don't want to be preachy, or anything, but you ought to cut a lot of this shit out." He indicated the glowing joint between his thumb and forefinger, before passing it back to Jo-jo. "You can fuck up your head and, you know, if you're not real careful he's gonna find out."

"I don't do any more than a lot of others."

"Tell him that."

Jo-jo shrugged, but reflectively, without bravado.

Hesitantly, Billy put his hand on his brother's shoulder. "I just don't want, you know, to see you get in trouble."

"Yeah, I know," said Jo-jo softly.

They fell into another silence, one too full of emotion for speech. Finally, Billy said, "Well, I guess we ought to turn in."

The next day Billy drove hard along the monotonous stretches of Interstate 95, punctuated only by square and rectangular green signs, bland as bureaucrats, telling them where they were. By early afternoon they arrived in Charleston, and found another motel with another tiny swimming pool.

"I guess we ought to see the school," said Bill. He sounded worried, as though he were afraid of being disappointed. From the desk clerk they got a map of the city, on which, limned in brown, was an area indicating the college. Following directions from the clerk—"You cain't miss it"—Billy drove past spired churches and porticoed houses, then continued westward through narrow nondescript streets until they came to an opened gate. A cadet, wearing

the summer uniform Billy recognized from the catalogue, stood by a guardhouse and watched them
with alert, curious eyes. He was tall and blond, and
stood straight.

"Is it all right to look around?" asked Bill def-
erentially through the window.

"Yes, *sir!*" replied the cadet smartly, stepping back
from the car.

Billy drove slowly into the enclosure. Beyond the
gate the avenue opened onto a large worn green
rectangle circumscribed by a paved and curbed road.
There were two cannon and a flag pole at one end,
and a tank and a missile pointed skyward at the
other. Oaks festooned with lacy Spanish moss lined
one side, and palmettos, their trunks padded with
rusk-like fronds, dotted another. Encompassing the
parade ground were grey and white buildings, bulky
and solid.

Boys were everywhere, walking purposefully across
the parade ground, strolling in relaxed clumps,
laughing, serious, saluting, running. They filled the
quadrangle, moved across and around it, inhabitants
of a self-contained empire, subject to laws and pas-
sions that were obscure to outsiders. As he drove,
Billy watched them, these cadets with stiff spines,
and uniforms that eliminated pimples, incompetence,
and shyness. He thought: *Soon I'll be one of them.*

Bill said, "This looks like the real thing."

"It's awfully pretty," said Harriet.

"What's that stuff hanging from those trees?" asked Evan.

Billy drove carefully past the massive, squat buildings, both hands on the wheel. Some of the boys looked unseeingly at the car, one of many travelling through the campus. As they came back to the gate, Billy speeded up.

"Yes, sir," said Bill reflectively, "that's the real thing, all right."

They returned over the next few days, squeezing in quick tours between bouts of sightseeing. "Why don't we scoot by the school?" Bill would say proprietarily, like someone who wants to make sure everything is running smoothly back at the shop. He scrutinized the buildings and students with a critical, satisfied eye: "They keep it in good shape," he would say, or, "They don't seem to have any slouches," or, "They really look like a great bunch of boys."

"They seem awfully nice," Harriet would agree.

Billy watched the boys, and wondered which ones would be his friends.

The night before he was to check in, Bill shyly asked his oldest son if he wanted to go for a little walk after dinner.

"Well, son," said Bill after a silence, "I guess tomorrow you'll be on your own. Sort of, anyway."

"Yeah," said Billy, embarrassed by the catch in his voice. He cleared his throat.

"I just want you to know, son, that your mother and I are awfully proud of you."

Billy looked into the clear depth of the pool filled with artificially blue water.

"I just wanted you to know that . . . uh . . . we love you."

"Me, too," said Billy.

Bill put his arm over his son's shoulders. "You have a chance to really make something of yourself. I'd give anything if I'd had your opportunities. You're going to have to work hard, but you can do it."

"Yeah. I know."

From his billfold Bill took a twenty-dollar bill. "Use this to treat your buddies," he said, as he pressed the money into Billy's palm.

Silently they returned to the motel and at the door of Billy's room, his father pulled him into a fleeting embrace. "Goodnight, son."

"Goodnight," Billy said, afraid his voice might crack again. Without meeting his father's eyes he slipped into the room he shared with his brothers.

The next morning he was excited yet melancholy as he drove the family to the campus. He pulled carefully to the curb in front of the grey three-storied barracks built around a blue and white checkered quadrangle, and skillfully parallel parked, using only one hand.

Other families were depositing their sons, and clusters of parents and siblings stood around their cars while luggage was unloaded, the one to be left behind apprehensive, curious, and eager among the nervous jokes and awkward caresses.

The Johnsons stepped onto the patchy grass, worn bare in spots, and stood uncertainly facing each other. Bill opened the trunk and hauled Billy's suitcases out. Though he knew where he was to go, Billy seemed unable to make the first move, but stood, arms at his sides, as though expecting to be led away. Bill was equally at a loss.

"What are we waiting for?" Jo-jo asked petulantly, embarrassed by the indecision.

Before anyone could answer, a tall, blond boy with bright white teeth and ingratiating, confident blue eyes, stepped into their midst and, holding out his hand to Bill, said, "Good morning, sir, I'm Corporal Jackson, and this is my barracks. Can I be of some help?" His grey, short-sleeved shirt was open at the neck, and the crisply pressed blue trousers had a black stripe down each leg. A blue-grey garrison cap was cocked over his forehead. "I'd like to welcome you all and show you around if I can be of some assistance." While shaking Bill's hand he managed to bow to Harriet and to take in the three boys with his glance. The Johnsons were mesmerized.

Billy shyly studied the apparition with awe and pride: this was what he would be in a year's time. Bill Johnson responded robustly: "How do you do, sir. Certainly glad to meet you."

"Just call me Ernest, sir, Ernest Jackson."

"Ernest, this is our son, Billy. He's going to be joining you. Heh, heh, heh."

Thrust into prominence Billy grew timid. "How do you do," he muttered. Jackson, with a radiant smile, clasped Billy's hand. "Mighty glad to have you with us, Billy. If you have any questions or need any help, don't hesitate a minute to let me know."

"Thanks," said Billy.

"Mother," Bill said to his wife, "It's good to know we'll be leaving our boy in such fine company."

"It certainly is," said Harriet, smiling at Jackson, who seemed to stand at attention. Evan watched him with open admiration, and Jo-jo muted his impudence.

"Is this your first time away from home, Billy?" Jackson asked, brisk but friendly.

"Yeah. Yes."

"If you need to know anything, you be sure to come to me, now, you hear?" His drawl was warm, his eyes honest.

"Thanks."

"After you get settled in, I'll show you around." He winked so quickly Billy thought he alone noticed.

Bill watched proudly. "I hope you boys aren't hatching trouble," he said playfully.

"No, *sir*," protested Jackson with a glint of mischief. They all laughed. "I've got to be getting on," he continued, and shook hands all around again. Just before striding off he said to Billy, "Now I mean what I say, you hear? You be sure to keep in touch." He marched away, the embodiment of a gallant tradition.

"He's a good friend," said Bill, "a good buddy to have."

"Such a gentleman," Harriet agreed. "A Southern gentleman. That's what you'll be, honey. It's the best kind."

"Yeah," said Billy, and he laughed self-consciously. Yet, he knew that what his mother said was true.

Jackson's visit galvanized them, and they gathered up the suitcases and trekked through the arch into the quadrangle of Billy's barracks. The interior court was ringed at three levels with verandahs onto which the rooms opened. Billy's room was on the second floor. Like the others it was small, spare, furnished with a double bunk, two dressers, two desks, two chairs, and a metal locker. The walls and floor were beige, as near to colorless as paint can get.

Billy was disappointed in his roommate, Sam, a gangly, shy boy from North Carolina who stood awkwardly at the periphery of the room and kept saying "Excuse me" as the Johnsons bumped into him.

Bill pronounced the room fine, and Harriet said it was nice. Then they walked out to the car together and Billy was afraid he might cry. He gruffly hugged his mother and manfully shook hands with his father; to his brothers he gave a casual wave. He stood at the curb as they pulled off, and was suddenly alone.

The other parents disappeared, and the only adults were men in military uniforms who always seemed to be in the distance. Suddenly the school was in the hands of boys. They were older than Billy, and sterner and intimidatingly authoritative, but they were only boys nonetheless. These were the buddies he had looked forward to meeting for the past year.

One of them, short and pugnacious, burst into his room and bellowed, "Attention!" Billy looked at him, unbelieving, and the boy, red in the face, screamed, "You snot-wad! You scum-bag! When I tell you 'Attention' I want to see you snap! What's your name?"

"Billy Johnson."

"Billy Johnson, *Sir!* Now, what's your name?"

Billy hesitated.

"What's your *name?*" shrieked the boy.

"Billy Johnson."

The boy's eyes bulged with rage. "You call me *Sir!* You call any upperclassman who deigns to notice a piece of shit like you *Sir!*" Then he left, as suddenly as he had come.

Billy was still trembling when another boy slammed open the door and yelled, "Attention."

He was herded at a trot from one building to the next. With the other freshmen he gathered uniforms, had his hair clipped so short the pink scalp showed through, and was ordered to the mess hall for a nauseatingly tense meal. Boys popped up from nowhere to harangue and insult him. He was forced to drop to the dirt and do push-ups until his arms gave out. And he had to run, run, run everywhere—

"On the *double!*" some adolescent voice would screech after a command. Sam was as apprehensive as he, yet seemed to take matters more in his stride. "Boy," he said, "they sure do carry on, don't they?" Billy, choked with outrage, did not answer. He could not understand why they were so vicious.

At the end of the day, dust mingling with adhesive sweat on his body, he crept into his room. Finally, he believed, there would be respite. He unpacked his new seersucker robe and rubber thong slippers, found his shaving bag, and went flop-flopping down the verandah to the head. The hiss of running showers and the boisterous, amicable shouts of other students reassured him as he edged into the flourescent-lighted room, where tendrils of steam hovered near the ceiling. The other boys were naked except for an occasional towel around the waist. He was suddenly ashamed of the red and white robe that had felt so crisp just minutes before.

Carefully avoiding the eyes of the others, he started toward the shower, untying the robe as he went.

A lanky redhead spoke with a nasal twang from the toilet where he sat unconcernedly in full view: "Looks like we got a faggot with that new batch."

The other freshmen were suddenly preoccupied with washing their faces and brushing their teeth. The sophomores, juniors, and seniors sized Billy up. He turned toward the redhead who sat on the white porcelain toilet, feet solidly planted on the concrete floor, elbows on his knees. "I'm not a faggot," he said.

A naked brown-haired boy, tanned mahogany except for a narrow strip of milky white groin and buttocks, skin still glistening from the shower, glared at him and bellowed, "You *what!*"

A hissing shower was turned off in the ensuing silence.

"You *what,* you shit-faced knob?" yelled the naked boy.

"I'm not a faggot," Billy repeated in a muted voice.

From the toilet where he sat, the redhead said, "I guess we gotta teach this Yankee faggot how to talk."

He felt ridiculous among the unclothed boys watching him. Nervously he took off his glasses and put them in his pocket. "I just came to take a shower."

The brown-haired boy grasped the nape of his neck and pushed his head toward the floor with a powerful thrust of his muscled arm. "When you talk to your betters you say *Sir.*" He continued pushing Billy's head until it almost touched the concrete floor. "Do you understand, scum bag?"

"Yes, Sir," said Billy, his voice muffled.

"Pop off, like you mean it."

"Yes, *Sir!*" Billy screamed, "Yes, *Sir!*"

"Gimme ten," demanded the brown-haired boy.

"Take that dress off first, faggot," said the redhead from the toilet.

"Yes, *Sir*!" He took off the robe and looked for a place to hang it. Without his glasses, walls and bodies blurred.

"Gimme twenty!" yelled the brown-haired boy. "Now!"

Helplessly he held the robe, looking for a hook.

"Hell," said the redhead, "this little peckered Yankee sure has got a lot to learn."

Someone giggled.

Into his ear the muscled, tan boy yelled, "Get down and give me thirty! *Now!*"

He fell to the clammy concrete floor and pressed his chest against it, his palms flat and arms raised by his ribs like the legs of a praying mantis. His shoulders ached and the concrete was slimy against his naked skin. He began to pump.

"Keep your butt down, faggot," said the redhead.

"Count off," yelled the naked boy.

". . . three . . . four . . . five . . ." he shouted after each effort. He had to stop twice. The second time the boy standing over him had stuck a toe in his ribs and said, "Finish up, shithead, or you'll give me another thirty."

Jerkily he completed the set, then lay still.

"Get up," yelled the boy, "and *brace!*"

He jumped to his feet, rigid, his chest expanded, his chin disappearing into his neck.

The redhead, still sitting magisterially on the toilet, said, "Next time, faggot, you say Sir, and you say it fast. Understand?"

"Yes, *Sir!*"

"Get to your bunk. On the double," said the muscular boy, thrusting the robe into his chest.

Naked, he had run from the head down the verandah and into his room, the robe flapping after him. He was still gritty with dust, and where he had lain on the floor his skin was smeared and pocked by concrete. Stunned, he crawled into his bunk.

He did not grow accustomed to the abuse. When Sam, who accepted indignities with, at most, a philosophical shake of the head, tried to joke about their lot, Billy would not respond. After a while he and Sam hardly spoke. Billy lived through days with his mind and spirit in suspension, like a part of the body that has been anesthetized by a blow. Then he began to resist.

He did not erupt. Instead, he grew surly, taciturn, and evasive, and crept around the campus, watchful and bristling, like a wounded dog. His hatred of his tormentors was invisible, but it went deep enough to inform his every action. He plotted even the simplest function, such as a trip to the head or going from one class to another, with them in mind, and prepared routes of escape and catalogued a battery of excuses to explain or mitigate his behavior. Instead of screaming his rage, he refused to polish his shoes; rather than outstaring an upperclassman, he let his shirttail flap loose. Such defiance brought him even more attention, and he accumulated demerits so rapidly that he became a joke among the freshmen as well as the older boys. Sam was embarrassed to be his roommate. When alone in their room, both would act as if the other did not exist.

There was no conscious plan to Billy's behavior, but expulsion was in the back of his mind. He never learned whether it would have come to that, for a chance encounter one evening in a bar changed his attitude.

Though just off the campus, The Sand Dollar Bar was out of bounds for all students. Against orders, Billy had slipped away from the barracks and walked there, not because he was thirsty for beer, but because he was desperate for companionship, even the illusory sort that can be had in a bar where he knew no one. As the smell of beer and stale smoke hit his nostrils, he saw Ernest Jackson hunched over the pool table in the back, half illuminated by the low overhanging light that shone on the green baize surface of the table and cast everything around it into shadows.

He had seen Jackson several times since his first day, but Jackson never appeared to remember him. The glimpses did not eradicate the first impression of golden, sunny, self-assurance Jackson had made. He always seemed to be smiling and offering his hand to be shaken. One evening in the cafeteria Billy overheard an upperclassman say, "That fucking Jackson is brown nosin' his way to an A in poly sci." The boy to whom he spoke shrugged and sneered, as if to say, "What did you expect?" Billy had been surprised to learn that someone might not like the boy who had so dazzled the Johnsons.

In The Sand Dollar, as he saw Jackson carefully aiming his cue at the brilliant white ball, Billy felt longing as potent as desire. Cautiously he surveyed the bar, certain that other cadets had to be there. After his eyes became accustomed to the gloom, however, he was surprised to see that Jackson was shooting pool by himself, tipping his can of Coors at ever more acute angles, and solemnly studying the array of pool balls. The only other people in the bar were a few locals.

Jackson finished his beer. When he came to the bar for another he stood just two stools away from Billy. After giving his order, Jackson glanced around the room with the air of someone who does not expect to see anything worth noticing. His gaze slid over Billy, then his eyes snapped back to him. "Hey, man," he said affably.

"Hi," said Billy.

"How's it going?" Jackson asked.

"Okay."

Jackson looked closer. "Oh, yeah," he said, surprised. "You're the guy. . . ."

"Billy Johnson."

"Yeah. Sure." Jackson extended his hand. "Good to see you."

Billy shook the hand.

"You a regular here?" Jackson asked.

"No."

"Have a beer on me." Before Billy could protest that he already had a can, Jackson had summoned the bartender and ordered.

"Thanks," Billy said.

"Shoot a little pool?" Jackson asked.

"I don't know how."

"Man, no time like the present," Jackson said, putting his hand on Billy's shoulder and guiding him to the table.

For the next hour they played, with Jackson giving Billy pointers on how to hold the cue and explaining which balls had to be pocketed first. Jackson was affable, faintly patronizing, and thoroughly at ease. He corrected Billy's stance and encouraged him with little pats on the back and shoulder and "Attaboy's" as they circled the table, bobbing over it, aiming their cues with their elbows pointing to the ceiling.

"Man, you're a natural," said Jackson. "In another couple of weeks you'll be beating the shit outta me."

"I don't think so," said Billy.

"Sure you will."

Jackson's nonchalant good fellowship at first piqued Billy's wariness. But as the evening wore on he was won over; three beers helped. Not once did they mention the academy. Billy forgot his troubles in a daze of clicking balls and drawled encouragements.

It was almost midnight when they returned to the barracks. Billy was surprised that Jackson swayed slightly, though his speech remained precise. "Man," said Jackson as they walked through the warm, humid night, "we're going to have to do this more often." He belched. "A man's gotta let off steam now and then. Right, ole buddy?"

"Yeah."

"One of these weekends we'll go into town and get laid. How about that?"

"Great."

Jackson put his arm heavily around Billy's shoulder. "I'll show you the ropes."

"Thanks."

They slipped through the parking lot fence where there was no sentry, and parted at the barracks; Billy said goodnight and stealthily climbed to his room, which was filled with the steady breathing of Sam.

Billy was not surprised the next day when Jackson did not appear to notice him. Nor was he upset, for public aloofness gave a greater cachet to their secret friendship. Billy slipped away again that week, but Jackson was not at the bar. He was caught sneaking back into his room and given demerits for having missed bed check. Instead of turning more surly and withdrawn, however, he spit-shined his shoes and made sure his trousers were creased. In his own mind he began to resemble the image of the cadet he had daydreamed back in New Jersey.

Billy hovered around Jackson but never called attention to himself. Jackson was always with people, always laughing, always shaking hands. Billy continued to detect an undercurrent of scorn for him, a slighting remark, a wink behind his back. "That fuckin' Jackson," a senior said. "He's just a natural ass-kisser." Billy had looked up surprised—he was brushing his teeth and was not wearing his glasses—for he thought the remark was addressed to him. But the senior was talking to someone on the other side of him, as though he were not there. The boy to whom the remark was addressed shook his head with a wry smile and contemptuously shrugged as he traced a swath down his cheek through shaving lather. "Full of bullshit," he said. "What the hell. Bullshit never hurt no one so long as you can spot it before you step in it."

They laughed, and Billy, for a few seconds, felt hollow and cowardly for not defending Jackson.

The following week Billy crept out again, even though he had been put on notice by his platoon leader. He carefully punched his pillow into human contours under the rumpled sheet while Sam pretended not to notice. He walked into the bar to find Jackson hunched over the pool table. Magically their first night was reproduced.

"Hello, ole buddy," Jackson greeted, sighting him along the cue. "We gonna have us a game, huh?"

"Sure," said Billy, happy for the first time since their last meeting. The shiny, slick, multicolored balls clicked and careened over the green baize, made brilliant by the naked bulb hanging above.

Billy loosened up. "I wish every hole I came up against was as easy to get into as that one," he said after sinking the eight ball which had been teetering on the edge of the pocket.

"Ole buddy," Jackson said, "some Saturday night real soon I'll show you a few holes a lot easier to get into than that one." He winked. "*Tight* but accessible, if you know what I mean."

"Yeah," said Billy.

"I guess you get a lot of pussy up North, huh?"

"Not really."

"Don't shit me, man." Jackson nudged him. "But believe me, you ain't seen nothing yet, like the man says. No pussy in the world's like Southern pussy. Ask anyone who's had some."

Billy smiled knowingly, his feeling of fraudulence diluted by Jackson's endorsement.

After that evening he had almost enough confidence to take some initiative. He thought about asking Jackson, when no one else was around, "When we gonna go get laid?" But he never worked up the courage. Though Jackson gladhanded everyone, he, like the other upperclassmen, treated the freshmen as a species apart. Billy took it as a sign of their friendship that Jackson never dressed him down like the others did.

Though he had started making more of an effort, Billy was still a target. Like the other freshmen he had been pummeled into physical conformity—the short haircut, the stiffened spine, the squared shoulders, the uniform—but he had not surrendered his autonomy. He resented such foolishness as learning "mess facts"—the answers to questions fired at freshmen during meals. "How many flag poles are on campus?" some senior would shout, or "How many bricks does it take to complete the big chimney?" Freshmen would scurry around the campus counting the limp flags hanging in the damp hot air or peer at the chimney through squinting eyes as their lips silently tallied the numbers. Billy would not join them.

From six in the morning until eleven at night he was supposed to be somewhere, to do something, to answer to someone. On weekends he had to work off demerits accumulated during the week by walking the silent tour in the quadrangle, his rifle on his shoulder, pacing back and forth over the blue and white checked courtyard with other cadets who had transgressed some rule. His rancor was kept in check by his secret friendship; he did not revolt.

Then on the Saturday before Thanksgiving he was wrenched from his illusion, the way a weed is yanked from the ground. Like a weed he withered.

The incident began no more significantly than hundreds of others happening to him and the other freshmen. A short bulldog of a boy ordered him to move some rocks that had been kicked onto the sidewalk from a border. Billy's uniform was clean and his shoes were shined; in spite of the heat he felt crisp and neat. Not bothering to disguise his anger, he slowly pushed a rock to the side.

"Faster, shithead!" the bulldog yelled. Behind him stood two other upperclassmen, monitoring him.

Billy disdainfully nudged the next rock with his foot.

"I said *move* those rocks, scum bag!" the boy yelled, his face red from embarrassment. Behind him the other upperclassmen impassively watched the performance of both. "I don't mean *play* with it like some faggot! I mean, goddam it, pick it up and *move* it!"

Billy paused to give him a sullen look, then turned to the next rock and languidly bent down to shove it to the side.

"You call that moving a rock? You half-assed fairy, you pick up the rock and take it off the walk! You understand?"

Billy said, "Fuck you." He picked up his books and walked away.

For an instant he felt a liberating exhilaration. It was quickly replaced by fear of reprisal, but none of the boys followed him as he walked toward his barracks.

The November heat was oppressive—moist and stifling—and the flags hung soddenly over the campus. The sun glowered on the broad expanse of parade ground ringed by palmettos and moss-hung oaks. Billy reached his barracks and passed into the courtyard. From the door of his room on the second gallery he glanced down at the cadets mindlessly pacing off punishment circuits from one end of the quadrangle to the other. He was sure he would be joining them soon.

He entered his room carefully, even though he knew Sam had a weekend pass. Caution had become a habit. No one was there. His shoulders slumped with relief as he removed his cap. Sweat trickled around the thick black-plastic frames of his glasses. He took them off and put them on the desk.

He crawled onto the top bunk and lay on his back, his eyes closed. He would have liked to sleep, but was too tense. He hummed the Duke's aria from *Rigoletto* as he jiggled his foot in rhythm.

"Tum tum te tum te tum," he intoned, barely moving his lips.

The door slammed open, a voice exploded, " 'Ten SHUN!" and bodies rushed into the room.

Without his glasses Billy could not make out the faces, but only the threatening forms surging toward his bunk.

"I said 'ten *shun*, you snot-faced piece of shit!" The voice bellowed with fury. A hand grabbed his arm and yanked him off the bunk. He landed on his feet, crouched near his desk, and instinctively reached for his glasses, fumbling them onto his face.

" 'Ten SHUN!" the voice yelled again, the mouth
only an inch from his face, spewing spittle and hot
breath. It belonged to the bulldog boy.

Behind Billy another voice screamed, "Brace, asshole! You already got ten demerits."

Even as he thrust out his chest, threw back his
shoulders, jammed his chin into his neck, he could
not help protesting, "What for?"

A fist slammed into his ribs. "For not coming to
attention fast enough, you snot-wad! And you just
pulled another ten for sounding off."

"You're never gonna learn, shithead," said the
short boy in front of him, glaring out of cold, satisfied
eyes as he thrust his face, reddened by melodramatic
anger, into his own. "You've fried your own ass,
knob."

Behind Billy a quiet, more reasonable voice asked,
"Johnson, did you tell Corporal Blaign here to com-
mit an impossible physical act upon himself?"

Billy hesitated.

"Pop-off, scum bag," screamed the fierce blue-
eyed Blaign.

"It wasn't . . ." he began.

"SHUT UP! Answer yes or no!"

Silently Billy struggled against his fear. Behind
him the rational voice repeated, more sternly, "Answer me, Johnson. Did you tell Corporal Blaign to
fuck himself?"

"Yes, sir, but . . ."

"SHUT UP!"

"Was that an intelligent thing to do?" asked the modulated, judicious voice.

"No, sir."

"Don't you want to be a cadet, Johnson?" The voice was so civilized, in contrast to the bawling enraged noise from the short boy in front of him, that he was grateful.

"Yes, sir."

"Sound off like you had some balls," said Corporal Blaign, his chin pugnaciously jutting toward Billy's.

"Yes, SIR!"

"If you want to be a cadet, Johnson, why do you keep fucking up?"

He didn't answer.

Blaign yelled into his face, "Why do you keep fucking up?"

"I don't . . . I mean, I . . ."

"You saying you don't fuck up?"

"Yes, sir."

The others snickered, and one said, "Just look at that wad of crap. Why aren't your shoes shined, shit head?"

"They are shined, Sir."

"You calling me a liar?"

"No, Sir."

"Why aren't your shoes shined?"

"I don't know, Sir."

"You're a slob. A disgrace to the battalion. Are you ashamed to be such a fucked-up, no-good shit head?"

"Yes, Sir."

"Pop OFF, scum bag," screamed Blaign into his face.

"Yes, SIR."

Then from behind him a soft, mellifluous voice said, "It looks like the Johnson family's raised their own turkey for Thanksgiving."

The others laughed. Billy did not want to believe that he recognized the speaker, and involuntarily twisted toward the voice.

"BRACE, asshole!" Blaign shouted, spraying his glasses with spit.

"How about that, slob," asked someone behind him. "You going home for Thanksgiving?"

"Yes, sir."

"How you going?"

"I'll fly, sir."

"Can Yankees fly? I didn't know Yankees could fly." Mock innocent tone, simulating curiosity.

"Fairies fly," said another, decisively.

"Same thing," said the first.

"Is a Yankee the same thing as a fairy?" Blaign yelled into his face.

"No, sir."

"He doesn't sound very convinced. Kind of wishy-washy. What do you think, Jackson?"

Smoothly, with honeyed vowels, Jackson pronounced, "Well, I think it's something we ought to test. Scientific like. Let's see if Yankees can fly."

Standing rigidly in the middle of them, Billy's face was hot with shame. His insides were dead at Jackson's betrayal of him.

"I've always wondered about that," said another, "but I never had the chance to find out."

"Here's your chance," said Jackson.

Suddenly they clutched his wrists and ankles, and he was lifted off the floor. He hung face down, struggling. For an instant he was suspended, disbelieving.

"Put me down," he said, raising his head, turning futilely toward Blaign. "Let me alone."

"Now altogether," said Jackson. "One!"

They swung him forward.

"Two!"

He was swept backward in an arc so steep his head pointed to the floor.

"And THREE!"

Flung like a rock from a slingshot, he smashed head first into the grey steel door of his locker. There was blackness for an instant—no sight, no hearing. Then ragged edges of feeling crept back into his senses. He was on his hands and knees, his head hanging over his glasses on the floor.

"Hell," said the quiet voice, "Yankees don't fly too good, do they?"

"This one doesn't."

"Does that mean he's not a fairy?"

"Not the kind that flies."

"There're other kinds of fairies," said Blaign, standing over him, arms akimbo.

"I guess," said Jackson gravely, "we will have to account this experiment a failure." He opened the door and stepped onto the verandah.

Blaign leaned over Billy before following the others. "Next time, shit face, you'll think twice about popping off to an upperclassman."

Billy stayed on his hands and knees as he cautiously felt for his glasses. When he picked them up the right stem flopped outward, then fell to the floor. He tried to fit the temple piece back onto the frame, but he couldn't see well enough to figure out just what was broken. Sitting on his haunches, he balanced the frame over his nose and anchored it with the endpiece behind his left ear. His fingers lightly grazed his forehead until he found a lump over his right eye. Carefully he circled and explored it, then looked at his fingertips. There was no blood. He remained crouched facing the locker, ashamed and guilty, for he knew that somehow he should have defended himself, should not have allowed this to happen.

On the verandah laughing voices moved nearer. Quickly he got to his feet, and sat at his desk with his back to the door. The boys passed without stopping as he stared at the blank tan wall.

From the desk drawer he took a roll of scotch tape, pulled off a strip, then removed his glasses and fitted the broken stem into the frame as best he could. Carefully he wound the tape around the joint until there was an opaque lump. He put the glasses back on and stared again at the wall.

His shoulders sagged. *Let's see if Yankees can fly.* Jackson's voice coated his mind like syrup. The pain stopped his breath.

Under the scotch tape was his plane ticket. The time between now and the Wednesday reservation gaped like a wound. He held the ticket and suddenly stood. Stuffing it in his pocket, he put on his cap and went resolutely to the door. Taking a deep breath he jerked the door open and looked up and down the verandah before stepping out. There were only the cadets below who continued their doleful trudging. He pondered whether to go to the phone in the barracks or to use one of the booths in the recreation building. A second's reflection persuaded him that the risk of a trip across the campus to gain privacy was preferable to a call from the open phone below where anyone passing could hear him. He hurried down the stairs and through the sallyport.

Cutting across the parade ground he passed the two howitzers flanking a flag pole and the monument to all graduates since the Civil War who had been killed in battle. Just the afternoon before, during the regular Friday review, he had stood here at attention facing the bleachers where a few tourists sat with their cameras and sunglasses to witness the student body impressively massed in battalions as bagpipes skirled and officers bellowed their commands. Such moments made his chest expand with pride. The two cannon had roared the salute, and dazzling white smoke engulfed the ranks of erect and serried boys. Then it dissipated into the humid sun-drenched air, and he and the others had marched off the field as tourists snapped pictures.

Now, he was grateful he was the only person crossing the patchy grass. Everyone else, he realized as he checked his watch, was in the mess hall across the campus. It suddenly became important to complete his calls and get back to his room before dinner was over. He dashed into the recreation hall, dialed the number, and asked for the next flight out. The sweet, friendly voice at the other end politely drawled a refusal: he could not leave that night, nor even the next day, because all flights were booked, and even if they hadn't been, the price he had paid was for a weekday flight. She was terribly sorry, and when did he want to go? Monday, he told her, as soon as possible. That would be just fine, she replied; he could leave at one o'clock, be at the airport at least a half hour before, and be sure to have a nice day.

He did not want to talk to his father. A telegram, he decided. He sent a terse message to meet him at La Guardia at five-thirty-two on Monday evening.

As he left the booth two freshmen came up the stairs. He avoided their eyes, but one of them, bluff and stocky, said, "Hey, boy, what's that on your head?"

Instinctively he felt the lump. "I hurt it," he said, without stopping.

The other grabbed his arm, and peered with exaggerated interest into his face. "You been bopped."

They were two friends from Georgia, and he had never spoken to them before. They knew what had happened. He could tell from their air of innocent concern, their menacing friendliness. He pulled back. "I hurt it," he repeated.

"Hell, you must of put your head in a cement mixer. Why'd you do a thing like that?" With amused curiosity the cadet scrutinized the lump.

"I have to go," he said.

"What's the rush?" Just below the surface of the question was a threat. They smelled his weakness. One of them gripped his arm, and both blocked his escape.

He was exhausted, and had no stomach for fight. "Look," he said, desperate to be alone, "I can't talk, now. . . ."

"Why not? You got pussy waiting back in your bunk?"

The other guffawed.

He yanked his arm free. "I've just had some news," he said. "My mother . . ."

They froze.

". . . my mother's dying of cancer."

The two gawked.

"Ah, shit," said the shorter cadet, in the awed voice of someone who has just seen a car wreck. "I didn't know. . . ."

"Hell, we didn't know," chimed in the other. "That's really tough, man."

He left them staring after him in embarrassment. In the foyer he stopped at the vending machine and bought three cheese sandwiches. Carrying the stack in his left hand, squeezing the soft white bread through the clear plastic, he rapidly returned to his barracks. The light was softer as the sun set, but the air was still hot. From the huge oaks ringing the parade ground the Spanish moss dripped unagitated by breezes. He rushed up the stairs two at a time to get to his room.

That evening and the next day he spent on his bunk. He rationed the cheese sandwiches, for he could not face the weekend mess hall with its cavernous vista of partially filled tables and the smell of Clorox. Cadets passed back and forth in front of his closed door, talking, laughing, trotting to appointments, kidding, insulting, calling to each other.

Late that evening he had to go to the head. As he stepped into the bright fluorescent rectangle he saw two cadets at the sinks and another showering. Without looking at them directly he went quickly to the furthest booth and used the toilet. As soon as he finished he started for the door and the safety of his room.

"Johnson," said one of the boys, a pock-faced senior named Burdelle.

"Yes, Sir." He stopped.

Burdelle dried his hands and came toward him, serious and concerned. "I heard about your mother, Johnson. That's really tough." He awkwardly touched Billy's shoulder and let his hand rest there. "If there's anything I can do . . . ."

"Thank you, Sir."

The other murmured sympathetically, "Yeah, that's really sad."

He hated them. Their sympathy was for their own benefit; it made them feel manly and solicitous.

"After Thanksgiving," said Burdelle, "come by and see me. . . ."

"I won't be back after Thanksgiving, Sir," Billy said.

Burdelle made a grimace as he slowly shook his head. "Jesus, that's tough. That's really tough."

"Thank you, Sir," he said, moving back so the senior's hand fell from his shoulder. Without expression he left the head.

When reveille sounded on Monday morning he rose, washed and shaved while avoiding the inquiring glances from other students. Instead of his uniform he put on jeans and tee shirt, and threw his laundry bag into his suitcase. Just before shutting it he studied the dress uniform he had worn so rarely, then took it off the hanger, folded it carefully and packed it.

He tucked the white cap in one corner, and his glossy black shoes in another.

His flight went through puckered, grey-tinged clouds, frozen turbulence that buffeted the plane as it thumped and swagged from side to side. His stomach was hollow, the same emptiness he had felt at school, as though fear had evacuated his belly. *Let's see if Yankees can fly.* Cautiously he felt the bruise, sneaking up on it with his fingertips.

The plane bumped to a landing, and he insinuated himself into the line of people patiently facing the front of the plane. The doors opened and everyone filed out as two flight attendants smiled and repeated mechanically, "Goodby, now. Have a nice day."

His family was waiting just beyond the corridor— father and mother shoulder to shoulder and, in front of them, Jo-jo and Evan—all squeezed into a square by an invisible border, as though grouped for a photograph.

He was embarrassed by his family's proud greeting. They were boisterously pleased to see him, so eager to show him off. They treated him as something he knew he was not.

Chapter Eight

O N FRIDAY NIGHT when Billy returned to Beaudale after his date with Wilma, his mother and father were sitting at the kitchen table, each with a half-empty cup of coffee. Bill was drumming his fingers, staring straight ahead, his lips pursed. Harriet, slouched over her cup, leaned her head on her hand, and looked worriedly at the sugar bowl.

"Did you see George?" his father demanded angrily.

"No. When?"

"Do you want some milk or juice, honey?"

"No."

"Just now. Tonight, while you were out."

"No."

"Did you have a nice time, honey?"

"Yeah."

Bill clicked his tongue in exasperation and heaved a sigh. "I'm gonna beat some sense into that little . . . jerk."

"Now, honey," said Harriet.

"What happened?"

Harriet looked sorrowfully at her son, but Bill continued to stare straight ahead, his fingers erratically twitching on the pale blue formica table top. "I hope you haven't been using any of that junk," he said.

"What do you mean?"

Bill slammed his hand on the table. "George has been smoking marijuana," he said furiously. "Have you?"

"No."

Nodding, confirmed in his trust, Bill said, "I knew you wouldn't let me down, son."

Abruptly he stood and walked to the drainboard. "Dammit! How could that kid do this to me? We've given him everything a kid needs." Self-pity colored Bill's voice as he said to Harriet, "What did we do wrong?"

"Nothing, honey," said his wife. At a loss, she added, "These things just happen, I guess. He's so young."

"He's old enough to know right from wrong! He's old enough to obey me! And I *told* him to stay in his room, and goddammit he walked out of this house just as big as you please. What can you do with a kid like that?"

"He'll come back, honey," said Harriet.

"I don't know if I'll let him in—by God I don't know if I want him here." He sat heavily and looked at Billy. "I've raised you boys to do the right thing and now that kid just kicks me in the face . . . he just spits on us."

Harriet shook her head mournfully and toyed with her cup.

"What happened?"

"I caught him red-handed! Sitting there on his bed and the room reeking of the stuff. He must think I'm some sort of dummy."

Billy dropped his eyes, and leaned awkwardly against the icebox.

"Your mother and I have made a lot of sacrifices for you kids," Bill said. "We've gone without a lot of things just so you boys would have everything other kids had. We've gone without vacations and new clothes and, hell, I don't know what all, just so you boys could get a leg up in the world. And this is how that little snot thanks us!" Bill flung his arms forward, as though he were casting out Jo-jo's betrayal. "And don't think I'm some sort of half-wit. Don't think I don't know he probably does more than just smoke marijuana. He's probably taking pills or worse. I've heard about these things. Do you know what all he's taking?" He looked at his son, trying to keep accusation from his eyes.

"No."

Bill shook his head. "No, he wouldn't have the nerve to tell you. Jesus!" He slammed his fist on the table. "It looks like we've got a bad apple." He laughed bitterly as he glanced at Harriet. "I've seen those hoodlums he hangs around with. Smart-alec little bastards. And that moustache—like a little hood, a little punk. That's where he picked up this crap. Their families don't give a damn."

"Oh, honey, now everything's going to be okay. Why don't you just have a talk with him. . . ."

Bill shrugged. "I'll tell you one thing, there are sure as hell limits to my tolerance. I'm no fool to sit back and let some little punk walk all over me. No sir. That kid's going to straighten up or he's going to get out."

"Well, honey, everything'll look better tomorrow morning. What are you boys going to do tomorrow?" Harriet asked, her sudden perkiness jangling like an unanswered telephone.

After a pause Billy said, "I don't know."

Bill sighed. "I was planning to go to the club for some target practice. I may not now though. I was going to take all you kids."

From the silence that followed, Harriet's voice sounded oddly chirpy as she asked, "How was Wilma, honey? Was she glad to see you?"

"Yeah, I guess so."

"And her mother?"

"Okay, I guess."

"Well, son," said Bill solemnly, "we're proud of you. I just want you to know that. Isn't that right, mother?"

"It sure is." Harriet smiled at them both and got up. "Let's all get some rest."

"Thanks," Billy said, and looked away.

By the next morning, Saturday, Jo-jo still was not home.

As Harriet, distant and perturbed, scrambled eggs, Bill sat grimly at the table in his robe, saying little, his anger dampened by worry. Evan looked mutely from one to the other, and seemed grateful when Billy entered the kitchen.

"Jo-jo's still gone," he said, trying to disguise his excitement.

"Do you have any idea where he might be?" Bill asked his oldest son.

"No."

Bill snorted. "He'll come home when he gets hungry enough."

"Don't forget your orange juice," Harriet said to Billy from the stove, but without enthusiasm.

At that moment Jo-jo sauntered through the back door into the kitchen. He looked tired, but wore a faint sarcastic smile. "What's for breakfast?" he asked with exaggerated nonchalance.

His family stared at him for a few seconds. Bill got to his feet, grabbed his arm and slapped him across the face. "What the hell do you mean, doing this to your mother and me?"

Jo-jo flinched. There were tears in his eyes but they did not dilute his arrogance. "I was with friends."

"What friends?"

"Just some guys." Jo-jo warded off his father's glare with a defiant smile, no less maddening for being nervous.

At the stove Harriet clutched her robe to her throat, and held the spatula coated with eggs suspended above the frying pan. Evan watched, fascinated. Billy realized that both he and his younger brother were at that moment in awe, not of their father, but of their brother, who dared to oppose him.

"Don't you try your smartass tricks on me, George," Bill blustered, still clutching his son's arm. "I'm still in charge around here," he said. "I'm your father, and by God, you better not forget it. Now, I want to know where you've been and who you've been with."

"I was just hanging out with some guys."

Bill flung rather than dropped his son's arm. "Go to your room, young man. And stay there until you can give me a straight answer. I mean it. I want you in that room until I say you can leave."

Jo-jo kept his eyes insolently on his father long enough to establish disrespect, then strolled out of the kitchen.

"By God, I won't put up with any smart alecs in my house," Bill said, his anger riddled and wobbly.

The others were silent, too embarrassed to look at him.

"Here's your eggs, honey," said Harriet. "You want eggs, too?" she asked Billy.

Before Billy could answer, his father said, with a burst of heartiness, "You bet he does. He needs his protein. We're going to do some target shooting today."

"Oh," said Harriet, "that'll be fun."

"Can I go too, daddy?" Evan asked eagerly.

All seemed willing to erase the day and start it over. "I guess so," Billy answered his mother, as his father said to Evan, "Well, I don't know, hotshot. You'll have to ask your big brother. This is his last day home, and what he wants, goes."

"Can I go with you?" Evan turned to Billy expectantly.

"I guess so."

"Can I shoot, too?" Evan asked his father.

"Well, we'll see. Not if you don't eat your breakfast."

"Maybe you'll change your mind and eat some eggs with Billy," said Harriet playfully, going back to the stove.

"No, thanks," Evan said politely, and sat straighter.

"Is there any last-minute stuff you need to get done?" Bill asked his son. "You got everything ready for the trip?" When Billy hesitated, Bill rushed ahead, "I mean, you're all packed and ready to go?"

"No."

"Well," said Bill, "It won't take long to throw your stuff into your bag, will it?"

For reply, Billy looked at his father stonily.

Bill ignored him. "After we get back from the range today your mother and I'll help pack. Be done in no time. Right, mother?"

"Right," Harriet sang from the stove. "Do you think you could wear your uniform to church tomorrow?" she asked gaily as she put Billy's eggs before him.

"No."

"Oh, honey, you're so handsome in your uniform."

"Make your mother proud, son."

"Prouder," corrected Harriet, giving Billy's shoulder a squeeze.

Billy felt himself sinking like a stone in the wash of his family's relentless cheerfulness.

"Can I go to the airport tomorrow?" asked Evan.

"We'll all go," said Bill.

With the cautious expression of someone edging near a brink, Evan asked, "Even Jo-jo?"

Annoyance dimmed Bill's good humor, but did not extinguish it. "We'll see," he said. "Well, Boy, what you say, you ready to hit a few bull's-eyes?" To Harriet, he asked, "You remember when I used to call you Jane, and Billy, Boy?"

"I remember that racket you made."

"The Tarzan yell," said Bill.

"What was that, daddy?" asked Evan.

"You never heard my Tarzan yell?"

"Show me."

"Oh, honey, don't start that, now."

"What's the Tarzan yell, daddy?"

Bill took a deep breath and opened his mouth, but looking at his wife, choked with laughter.

Harriet put her hands on Billy's shoulders and said to him, "What are we going to do with these kids, honey?"

Billy stood. "I . . ." He looked at his plate. "I'm finished." His abruptness was a glacial spritz that froze the others.

Bill recovered quickly, stood and said, "Well, I guess then we'd better get moving. Right, son?"

"Yeah."

"Me too," said Evan.

Harriet, her hand at her throat, looked at her husband. "What about Jo-jo?" she asked softly.

Bill set his lips and said, "He's to stay in his room." Turning to Billy heartily, he asked, "You all ready? You gotta give your old man time to take a quick shower and shave. Fifteen minutes. No more." He bounded out of the kitchen.

"Well," said Harriet, "you should have fun."

Billy turned from her and Evan said, "Maybe I can shoot."

"It's up to your father," said Harriet. To Billy's back she said, "This should be fun for you, honey."

Billy left the kitchen without answering.

Twenty minutes later Bill was waving goodbye to Harriet, who stood at the door while Billy backed the Cobra out of the drive.

Evan, squeezed between his father and brother, excitedly asked, "Can I steer?"

"No," said Billy.

"Can I steer, daddy?"

"No, son, your brother's in charge."

"Can I shoot?"

"We'll see."

Billy drove silently, weaving carefully among the Saturday morning traffic, now swollen with early Christmas shoppers. A plastic Santa Claus or occasional string of unplugged colored lights looked incongruous in the brilliant autumn morning.

The first time Billy had made the trip to the Hilltop Pistol Range he had been younger than his brother, and even more excited. He was four, or a little older. Like Evan, he had wanted to shoot the guns, and his father had laughingly sat him on the waist-high shelf in the booth facing the target, had put the heavy ear plugs over his ears, and had covered his small hand over the trigger with his own. Behind them other shooters, men and women, had watched approvingly, saying, "That a way to go, Bill, start 'em young." "You gonna have one tough little kid there." "Nobody's gonna mess with *that* boy." His father had squeezed the trigger slowly, and Billy had been agonized with apprehension and excitement.

The shot exploded, unexpected, shocking every fiber of his body, stunning him. He had cried.

"Don't be a crybaby," his father had said as Billy, ashamed and frightened, had bawled all the louder.

"Poor little feller," said a woman.

"Now, son," said Bill, impatiently, bouncing him up and down in his arms and patting his back, "there's nothing to cry about. You're not hurt. Where does it hurt? Huh?"

It did not hurt, which made his tears all the more reprehensible. He was crying for no reason that he could explain, yet he could not stop. More painful than the fright was the embarrassment and disappointment of his father.

Billy had not thought of that day for a long time, but Saturday morning, as he drove to the club, it came back to him, and the memory carried its potent spurt of shame. He gripped the wheel with both hands until it passed.

"Boy, this part of the county is sure building up," Bill said. "In a few years, real estate's going to double."

After a pause Evan asked, "Is that good?"

"Sure," Bill said. "People with property will be better off."

"Will we be rich?" asked Evan.

Bill laughed. "Don't count on it. But we'll get by—like we've always done. Right, son?"

"Yeah," said Billy.

"What's it like down there at school? People seem to be doing okay?" Bill asked.

"I guess."

Bill's cheerfulness hung over the front seat like a plaintive question. Billy drove stolidly with his eyes on the road. He had traveled the route often, nearly always with his father, and with an anxiety that was at times so elusive it seemed a mirage, and at other times so massive it enveloped him. Each session was a contest.

The lessons had started when Billy was twelve years old. His father had said solemnly, "I think it's time you learned to handle these, son," as he cleaned his guns in the living room. The smell of the oil was sharp in his nostrils, and the black barrel of the pistol gleamed dully in the lamplight. "We'll go out to Hilltop on Saturday morning and you can shoot off a few rounds."

Harriet had been perturbed. "I don't know, honey," she said doubtfully. "Isn't it sort of . . . early. . . ."

"No," her husband replied firmly. "I've seen kids younger than him out there, and they're damn good shots. Billy is big enough to handle a gun."

Billy listened with a mixture of anticipation and fear. His father turned to him.

"You want to learn to shoot, don't you, son?"

"Sure," he said, his eagerness forced, yet not false.

"See there," said Bill to Harriet. "We've raised a real boy here."

"If you think it's okay." She smiled at Billy. "You be careful, now, honey."

At the range for that first lesson tension made Billy boisterous.

"Let me shoot it, daddy," he demanded when Bill carefully took the .22 caliber target pistol out of the leather carrying case.

"Now just a second, son." Bill was stern. "You have to be very careful with guns. You could hurt yourself or someone else if you're not." And he had enumerated the safety measures: Always consider a gun loaded, never point it anywhere but at the target.

The list seemed endless, and Billy was impatient. He became peevish. "Yeah, yeah," he said, interrupting his father. "Just let me *shoot* it, daddy. I'll be careful."

Bill compressed his lips. "You're not as smart as you think you are, son. You can learn from the experience of others."

Billy pouted as his father droned on; he fidgeted and mimed his boredom. By the time the gun was given to Billy, both of them were on edge.

Billy held the gun in one hand, arm straight away from his body, and pointed it at the target.

"That's not the way, son," said Bill with asperity. "There's a right way and a wrong way to do things, and that's the wrong way for you to hold a gun."

"That's the way I want to shoot it," said Billy. This was the stance he had seen in movies.

"That's not the way it's done."

"It's the way I do it."

"Dammit, you're just being pig-headed. Now, listen to me, and do what I tell you, or we can forget this whole thing. I mean it. If you don't straighten out, you'll go back to the car and wait for me there."

Billy's lip quivered and his father glared; after a few seconds of silence, Billy let his arm fall by his side.

"Now, then," said Bill, "You take the gun with *both* hands to hold it steady, and you stand this way, with legs far enough apart to give you a base"—he moved his son's legs where he wanted them—"and you aim like that." He looked at Billy critically. "Put one hand over the other . . . that's right. Now then. *That's* the way to shoot a pistol."

Billy sulked. This was not the way cowboys and gangsters did it.

"Why can't I do it the way I want to?"

"Because, dammit, it's not *right!* Go ahead, just go ahead. Here. Put on the ear plugs, and shoot it your way. You'll see what I mean." His father moved angrily to clamp the heavy sound deadeners over his ears. "Now, then, go ahead and shoot it like you damn well please," he yelled.

Suddenly, Billy no longer wanted to be like the movies. "I'll do it like you want me to, daddy," he said.

"No, no," Bill yelled. "Go ahead. See how smart you are. Go ahead and shoot it your way. Go on. Don't take all day." Bill's mouth was a grim line of anger.

"I don't want to," said Billy, close to tears.

"I'm losing patience with you, Billy."

Billy was suddenly afraid of the gun, afraid that if he flouted his father this way, something terrible would happen. He tried to recreate the stance his father had taught him, but Bill would not permit it.

"No, dammit," Bill yelled. "Go ahead and shoot it like *you* want to. Go ahead!"

Nervously Billy held the gun at arm's length and pulled the trigger. It recoiled and the cartridge flew over his shoulder.

"Ha!" said Bill. "You didn't even hit the target. *Now*, do you see why you were wrong? Didn't even hit the *target*."

"I'm sorry, daddy," said Billy.

"Now maybe you'll listen when someone tries to tell you something."

Abjectly, Billy stood with his legs well apart, arms extended, hands on the butt and index finger curled carefully around the trigger.

He became a good shot. Within a year he was punctuating the target's center more often than not. After a while he could even change his stance, bring it in line with his original desire, but by then it no longer mattered. Usually he shot the way his father taught him.

As the Cobra pulled into the lot only two cars were parked beside the low squashed building painted a dull, unevenly faded red.

"Not too crowded," said Bill.

Billy pulled into a space near the free-standing sign that proclaimed *Hilltop Rifle and Pistol Range*, and in smaller letters *Licensed Dealer, Civilian Defense, Target Shooting* and in still smaller script *By appointment only*. The owners, Sophie and Bob Arbuckle, had added the last in order, as Bob said, "to keep out the kooks."

As they got out of the car they could hear the sharp pop of target pistols muted by the walls separating them from the range. Bill carried the leather bag with the pistols, and Evan ran ahead to open one of the double doors that was covered with cracked clear varnish.

The room was small and crowded. Along one wall was a glass counter displaying leather mittens, safety glasses, ear plugs, and near that a row of vending machines dispensed coffee, cokes, sandwiches and candy bars. Four grey metal tables stood in the middle of the floor, each surrounded by an ill-assorted cluster of chairs: plain wooden kitchen-type, folding, and one typist's chair on rollers, with stuffing showing through the green plastic seat. Strewn on the tables were old copies of the *National Rifleman*, glossy, colorful, and slick. The wall at the far end of the room facing the door was half glass, through which the shooting booths and target range were visible. Wreathing the window was a skimpy string of tinsel, tarnished and worn from repeated storage, and from the tinsel dull red and blue balls hung at haphazard intervals. Near the door leading to the range a plump smiling woman with carefully beehived brown hair and large glasses with blue plastic frames sat at one of the tables cleaning a dismantled pistol.

"Hiya Sophie," said Bill jovially. "I see you're ready for Christmas."

"Hello, Bill," she said in a small, sweet voice, as she glanced complacently at the decorations. "Yep. Got that out of the way. Who's that stranger with you?"

"Hi, Sophie," Billy said.

"It's sure good to see you." She got up to kiss Billy's cheek and hug him. "You are getting so *big*. Bill, he's gonna be whupping you pretty soon."

"Not for a while. I'm still the boss. I pay the bills."

"What happened to your head?" Sophie asked Billy.

"He got into a rough game with a bunch of rebels."

"Well, I'd sure hate to see what *they* look like." She squeezed Billy's arm again, and then turned to the clipboard on the table, all business. "I guess you'll want two booths?"

"Yep. I'm gonna share mine with the hotshot here," said Bill, winking at Sophie as he put his hand on Evan's shoulder. Evan smiled shyly.

"Pretty soon you're gonna have a whole army."

"I've already got a whole army—at least that's what it seems like when I get the grocery bill."

Sophie and Bill laughed.

"Okay, numbers 10 and 11," said Sophie, briskly looking at her clipboard.

"Where's Bob?"

"Oh, he's in the city for a match. Be back tonight." To Billy, she added, "How long you gonna be here?"

"He's gotta go back tomorrow. He's gotta straighten out those rebels," his father answered.

"Well, now, he's just the boy can do it."

Billy's smile was strained. He stared at the range where three men sporadically fired, the sharp retorts softened by the glass wall.

"Well, boys, I guess we're ready. You got the guns, Billy?"

"Yeah."

Bill took a sheaf of targets from the table where Sophie sat and opened the door just as one of the other members fired a round; the blast made Evan wince. Billy passed around earplugs, then took his place in the booth shaped like a small closet with two walls missing, and a shelf built waist high. To his right was a handle connected to a pulley from which a clip hung. Billy attached his target, and cranked it to the end of the gallery. It fluttered in transit, then hung smooth, presenting the silhouette of a man in a business suit with a bull's-eye etched on his chest.

"Let's see how rusty you've gotten," Bill yelled to pierce the ear plugs. Billy did not show that he had heard. The Smith and Wesson was already loaded, and he aimed and fired. Unhurriedly, he fired again and again, standing solidly, his face frozen into concentrated impassiveness. He put the gun down, cranked the target back to the booth, and unclipped it. The center, where the silhouette's chest had been, was ripped into a gaping, tattered hole.

Bill, looking over his son's shoulder, yelled, "By golly, that's pretty good!"

One of the other men on the range joined them and clapped Billy on the shoulder. "That's some shooting, young man." He was tall and thin, and wore a red checked wool shirt.

Bill smiled at the man. "Looks like a few months of college has improved his aim. He probably thinks he's gonna outshoot his old man."

Billy, still facing the range, reloaded the pistol.

"Well, now, he just might at that," yelled the man pleasantly.

Bill's smile was fixed as he continued to study the target with its near perfect score. "Let me have the Smith and Wesson," he said.

"When can I shoot, daddy?" Evan asked.

Bill appeared not to have heard him. He took the gun into his booth and sighted his target. Carefully he shot a round, squeezing the trigger each time with concentration. He reeled the target in, and unclipped it; the silhouette's gut was like a sieve with jagged holes clustered around the bull's-eye.

"Close, but no seegar!" yelled the amiable man who had watched behind him. To Billy he shouted, "Looks like you outshot your old man."

"Did Billy win?" asked Evan, shouting like everyone else.

"Hush, son," snapped Bill. "It wasn't a contest." He continued to study his target, as though trying to improve the results.

The man winked broadly at Billy. "But if it *had* been a contest, you'd of won." He grinned at all of them, then ambled back to his own booth.

Bill glared at the man's back, then shook his head in disgust. "Let's try with the Ruger," he said shortly, handing it to Billy without meeting his eyes. "I'm a little rusty."

His father's abruptness dredged a familiar hole in Billy's gut, and he took the gun reluctantly. He hesitated, holding it barrel down.

Impatiently, Bill said, "Come on, son. What are you waiting for?" He stood behind the booth, arms crossed on his chest.

Billy attached a new target and sent it rippling to the end of the gallery. Then he took his stance, both arms extended, and fired. Tenseness made him linger over his aim. He was aware of his father behind him, watching and judging. When he had finished his round, he drew in the target; two shots had strayed to the outer edges of the target, and the other four were peppered around the bull's-eye.

Bill looked at the target without comment, and took the gun into his booth. He shot with even more care than before and twice lowered the gun a second to rest his arms before aiming again. Billy stood by Evan and watched his father without expression. When he was finished, Bill pulled in his target, and smiled as he held it up. All his shots were within the center ring.

"Did you lose?" Evan asked Billy.

"Shut up."

"Don't be a poor sport, son," Bill yelled gravely.

"How'd you do?" asked the man in the red checked shirt, returning to address his question to no one in particular.

For answer Bill held up his target. "I can still show my kid a thing or two," he said.

"Pretty good," said the man, nodding agreeably. Then he turned to Billy. "You gonna let your old man get away with that?"

"I guess he doesn't have much choice," said Bill, restored to good humor. Affectionately, he punched Billy's shoulder. Billy, a forced smile at the corner of his lips, stood with his arms hanging at his sides.

"When can I shoot, daddy?" Evan asked with as much whine as he could work into a shout.

"Well, how about right now?" To the man in the checkered shirt he added, "You can't start 'em too young."

"That's right," the man agreed pleasantly, and left the range.

Bill took Evan into his booth and gave him the Smith and Wesson. "Now, son, you already know the safety rules. Right?"

"Yes," said Evan doubtfully.

Billy watched his father crouch until his head was even with Evan's. "Okay," said Bill, "now you hold the gun like this," he enfolded his son as though he were a mold encasing a replica of himself, "and you aim like this . . . . Then you *slowly* squeeze . . . ." The shot rang and the target at the end of the range jumped.

"By golly, you got 'im," said Bill excitedly. He turned to Billy. "Your little brother's gonna catch up to you before long."

Billy did not acknowledge the remark.

Bill turned back to Evan, and guided him through five more shots.

Evan was excited and flushed as he pulled in his target and examined it. "How did I do, daddy?" he asked.

"Terrific," said Bill. "By golly, you'll be beating your brother and me before long."

Evan thrust the target at Billy who, with a glance, pronounced, "Great."

"Well," said Bill, "I guess we ought to be getting back or your mother'll be worried. You ready to go, son?"

"Yeah."

"Think this'll keep you sharp until you get home for Christmas?"

Billy looked away. Cautiously his father studied him an instant before gathering up the leather sack and putting the guns in it.

Evan still carried his target, and when he stepped from the range into the club room where Sophie was sitting, he shyly showed it to her.

"You do that? My goodness." She favored Bill with a motherly smile. "Your boys all got lots of talent." To Billy, she added, "I heard you been shooting up a storm out there."

"I did okay."

"He even managed to outshoot his old man. Once," said Bill, putting his arm around Billy and giving him a squeeze.

"Where's your other boy," Sophie asked. "Haven't seen him for a while. Now there's a good shot. Gonna be a champion, that one. Hope he's okay?"

"He's fine," said Bill heartily. "He's been grounded for a while today, for acting up a little, but he's fine."

"Spare the rod and spoil the child," said Sophie.

"Well, we don't have that problem," said Bill.

"I can see you don't," said Sophie emphatically. "I just wish all the kids came in here were as well behaved as yours." She turned back to her clipboard.

On the drive home Evan sat in the middle again, his target rolled into a baton which he held upright on his lap. Billy drove with sullen concentration, and Bill looked out his window and whistled tunelessly through his teeth.

"If this weather holds you're gonna have a nice day for traveling tomorrow," said Bill cheerily when they were half way home.

"Is it fun to fly?" Evan asked after a pause.

"It's okay," said Billy.

"Boy, when I was your age," said Bill, "I'd have given my right arm to ride in an airplane."

"I want to go in one, daddy."

"You will, one of these days," said Bill.

"Were you afraid?" Evan asked his brother.

"No."

"What's there to be afraid of?" asked Bill. "Safer than cars. Right, son?"

"I don't know."

Billy pulled into the driveway, shut off the ignition, and left the car without looking back. He was halfway to the house by the time Bill and Evan had gotten out. Harriet was standing at the door.

"Did you have a good time, honey?" she asked, but looked worriedly over his shoulder at her husband.

"It was okay," said Billy.

"We had us quite a day, mother," Bill called from the car. "We're getting to be a regular army of sharpshooters."

"I got to shoot," said Evan.

Harriet smiled, distracted. When Bill reached her she said, "Jo-jo left."

"Where'd he go?" asked Bill, surprised out of his good humor.

"I don't know. He just said he wanted to see some friends. I told him he'd better stay in his room, but he just left." Harriet was almost tearful behind the sparkle of her glasses. She nervously pushed her hand through her hair.

"Well, by God, that's the final straw." Bill's face was suffused with blood and he stood holding the leather bag of guns. Billy watched him, silently goading with his eyes. Evan looked from his mother to his father, frightened. "By God," Bill repeated, and slammed into the house.

"What's daddy gonna do?" Evan asked in a small voice.

"Nothing, honey," said Harriet. "Everything's going to be okay. Did you have a good time?"

From inside Bill called, "What time did he leave?"

"About half an hour ago."

Billy went into the house and up the stairs to his room. On his bed Harriet had neatly piled all the clothes he had brought with him from school; they had been washed and folded and smelled of detergent. Tee shirts, jockey shorts, socks rolled into neat little balls, blue jeans—ready to be packed for the trip back. He glared at the laundry an instant before wiping it off the bedspread with a sweep of his arm. He flopped on the bed on his back where he lay rigidly, his hands behind his head, staring at the ceiling.

Evan, still carrying his rolled-up target, came timidly to his door. "Daddy's really mad," he said hesitantly. "What do you think's going to happen to Jo-jo?" he asked with a mixture of anxiety and anticipation.

Billy shrugged.

Evan sighed histrionically, keeping his eye on his oldest brother, trying to attract his attention. He unrolled his target. "I'm going to put this on the wall next to Jerry's pennant. Do you think that's a good idea?"

"Yeah, if you want to."

Evan edged closer to the bed and sat gingerly, trying to ingratiate himself. He looked at the clothes strewn on the floor. "Is this all stuff you're taking back?" When Billy did not answer, he asked, "What's it doing on the floor?"

From downstairs they could hear their father's voice, but could not understand what he was saying.

"Boy," said Evan, "Daddy's really mad. Are you sorry to be leaving?"

"Haven't you got something to do?"

Evan was still for an instant before his face scrunched. "I was just trying to talk to you," he said. "But I guess you're too *important* to waste time with me." He slammed the door as he left.

With the door shut, Billy could not hear his father and mother below, but the tension created by Jo-jo's disappearance seeped over the sill like an odorless gas. He lay stiffly, his jaw clenched. He was not surprised by the knock on the door.

Bill stuck his head in the door at his son's barked invitation. "Resting up?" he asked in a careful voice. He appeared to have left his anger below, waiting at the door to trounce Jo-jo when he showed up.

"No. I'm not tired."

"Just relaxing, huh. I guess you don't get much chance to do that down there."

Billy stared at the ceiling.

"I guess they keep you pretty busy." Bill hesitated, then rushed on. "I think I'm gonna have to find something like that for George. I don't mean I can send him down there with you—even if they'd have him—but I think he's too much for your mother and me. We can't do anything with him. And now this dope thing. My God, who'd have ever thought one of my kids would end up taking dope."

Billy did not look at his father.

"I know you're close to George," Bill said. "I know he listens to you."

Billy lost his sternness as he looked questioningly at his father. "You mean you want me to talk to him?"

Bill frowned thoughtfully. "I don't know whether talking will do any good at this stage of the game. Sure, talk to him—if he gets back before you leave tomorrow. But setting an example—that's what's important, son. Show him by example how he should behave. Maybe you could write him more often from school—keep in closer touch."

Billy blinked. "Dad. Please don't make me go back."

His father had the look of a man who has been kicked when he's already down; surprise, disappointment, exasperation, bewilderment—all skittered in succession across his face as he stared at his son. His lips moved wordlessly before he said, "I thought we had this all settled. What's got into you?"

Billy shook his head. "You don't listen to me. It's never been settled. I can't go back because . . . I hate it there."

"But, we decided you'd at least give it a year." Bill raised his voice, as though sheer volume would make his son see reason.

"You decided that! I didn't decide anything."

"What a time to spring this on me and your mother. As if we didn't already have enough to worry about."

"But I've said all along—ever since I got home— I've said I can't go back."

"And, dammit, I say you *will*," Bill yelled.

Bill stood indecisively at the door, staring at the rigid quiet boy on the bed as though willing him to come to his senses. He started to go, then stopped and, like a runner getting his second wind, spoke in a more reasonable, but no less intense, voice:

"Listen, son, you're making too much of this. My God, it's a *college* you're going back to. You're so damned lucky to be there. I'd have done anything to have what you have now when I was your age. You think you're unhappy? Someday you'll understand how lucky you are to have me and your mother to give you opportunities that a lot of kids never get—that, damn it, *I* never got, you can believe me." He paused, watching his son anxiously. "You'll come out of there with some terrific buddies, and you'll be able to write your own ticket, get any kind of job you want. And you'll have a degree that counts for something."

Billy did not look at him.

"Son, your mother and I have given you and your brothers a family life that most kids never have . . . that I, God knows, never had. We've gone out of our way to do our best for you kids. I can't tell you how much it hurts when you and your brother turn around like this and just spit in our faces for our trouble."

Billy's jaw stiffened. "I'm not dealing drugs," he said.

Bill looked confused. "That's serious. That would be serious, it's true. But there are other ways to be ungrateful. You just think about that, son. You just give that some thought."

Billy turned to gaze out the window.

"You're already homesick," Bill said, "and, believe me, son, I can understand why. But just look at it this way. As much as you're going to miss your home, that much more you're going to appreciate it when you get back for Christmas." He dropped his voice. "Just think of how great the Christmas holidays are going to be. They're only a month away, son." From the door he looked compassionately at Billy, and nodded understandingly. "Some day, believe me, you're going to thank your mother and me for what we've given you."

Chapter Nine

BILLY LAY ON HIS BED most of the afternoon. He listened to the opera broadcast, tapping his fingers on the brown bedspread in distracted time to the music. Evan walked into the room once, wearing a pained and resentful expression. "Excuse *me*," he said, "but I lost my ruler. Maybe it's in here."

"That's okay."

Evan looked on the bureau and desk, barely grazing their surfaces before he turned back to his brother and hesitated. "What's that?" he asked, indicating the radio.

"Marriage of Figaro."

"You like it?"

"Yeah."

Evan hovered near the door, waiting for a sign of welcome, but Billy continued to stare out the window.

"I don't want to *bother* you," said Evan, and left, not quite slamming the door.

Once Billy heard his father's angry voice, and he thought that Jo-jo had come home. He did not care. His mother came to his room to see if he needed anything for the trip tomorrow. She looked at the clothes he had shoved to the floor, and then at his listless form. Her forehead creased as she asked, "You feeling all right, honey?"

"Yeah. I'm okay."

She picked up the clothes and stacked them on the desk.

"You need help packing?"

"No."

She went to the closet. "You look so terrific in your uniform. I hope you'll wear it to church tomorrow. Pretty please?"

The opera was finished, but Mozart was still coming from the radio, gay and brilliant. Billy's foot wiggled in tempo, and he did not answer.

Harriet sighed and smiled wryly. "All my boys are acting up today," she murmured. "Anything special you'd like for dinner?"

"No."

She felt his forehead. "I do believe that nasty bump looks a little better. Does it hurt?"

"No."

She smiled flirtatiously. "I've got a little surprise for you for dinner tonight," she said in the singsong voice used to beguile children. When he still did not answer she asked, "Don't you want to know what it is?"

"Yeah, sure," he said indifferently.

"Well, I'm not going to tell you. Then it wouldn't be a surprise." Mocking her own playfulness, she laughed.

Billy continued looking out the window.

"What are you going to do tonight?"

"Nothing."

"Not even going to see Wilma?" she teased.

He shook his head no.

"I'm sorry you're down in the dumps." She hesitated.

He looked at her resentfully.

"Well, honey, this is something for you and your father to work out. He wants what's best for you. So do I." She brightened. "I bet it'll be fun on the plane."

He looked out the window.

Harriet, standing at the door, cheerily admonished, "You get a little rest now, honey. It'll do you good," and then she left.

The music had given way to the news and he switched stations, still lying on his back, turning the dial idly through stripes of sound until he found another classical station.

He turned on his side. *Looks like the Johnson family raised its own Thanksgiving turkey.* He could hear the voice, smooth, honeyed, warm with humor. *My mother has cancer,* in his mind's ear, was like a screech, a craven whine. He turned on his other side to escape the memory. The radio played Chopin.

Evan called him to dinner with aggrieved abruptness. Billy descended to the dining room, where his mother and father awaited him expectantly. In the center of the table was a large cake with white icing.

"Surprise!" his mother said, pointing to it. "Didn't I tell you I'd made a surprise for you?"

"Your mother baked it herself," said Bill.

"With a little help from a Pillsbury mix," added Harriet.

Bill hugged her, then stood with his arm around her shoulders and they both beamed at Billy. "Just a little farewell party," said Bill gaily.

Harriet had set the table with the candles left over from Thanksgiving, though she had used the everyday pottery and glasses. There were only four places.

"Where's Jo-jo," Billy asked.

Bill frowned. "We won't worry about him now. This is *your* party."

"Yeah," Billy persisted, "but what's happened to him?"

"I don't know."

"You mean you don't know where he is?"

"No. He'll be home when he gets hungry enough." Bill was grim as he held the chair for Harriet.

"Sit down, honey," she said to Billy. "You have to eat your salad before you can have your cake."

"What kind of cake is it?" Evan asked.

"That's part of the surprise," Harriet teased.

"Is it chocolate?"

"Eat your dinner, then you'll find out."

Billy noticed that they had forgotten to light the candles. He took his place and silently dipped a spoonful of mashed potatoes onto his plate.

"Well, son," said Bill cheerfully, "by this time tomorrow you'll be back in Dixie. Do they call it Dixieland?"

"No."

Bill rushed ahead, chattering to Harriet and Evan. "When I was in the army those old boys from the South sure did talk about Dixie. Us from the North—some of us—called *them* rednecks, but not to their faces."

"Why, daddy?" Evan asked.

"I don't know. I guess because they were sun-burned from plowing the fields. It gets awfully hot down there, doesn't it, son?"

"Yeah."

"They're great people, though, the Southerners."

"They're so polite," said Harriet.

"They talk funny," said Evan.

"Well, to them *you* talk funny, just remember that," said Bill. "Isn't that right, son?"

Billy nodded.

The phone rang.

"You answer it, and tell them we're having din-ner," Bill said to Evan, who was already out of his chair and running to the hall. He returned almost immediately and took his seat. "It was for Jo-jo," he said.

"Who was it?" Bill asked sharply.

"I dunno. Just a guy. Asked for Jo-jo." Evan was apprehensive, as though he had betrayed someone.

Bill nodded grimly. "That young man's going to have a lot to answer for."

The table was silent, waiting for the return of good humor.

To help it along, Harriet cheerily asked, "Does anyone want any seconds?"

"Why aren't the candles lit?" Evan asked.

"Why, honey," Harriet laughed, "we forgot the candles."

"Well," said Bill, jumping to his feet, "It's never too late." He went to the kitchen and came back with a box of matches.

"Has everyone had enough?" Harriet asked.

"Well, I certainly had my fill," said Bill heartily, sitting down again. "Except I guess I'll just try a little piece of Billy's cake."

"Are we all ready for dessert?" Harriet asked brightly.

"Yeah," said Evan.

Harriet ceremoniously rose and brought back cake plates and a knife. Carefully she cut a wedge and gentled it onto a plate.

"The first piece is for Billy. It's his cake."

"I don't like chocolate," Billy said impassively.

"Oh, honey," said Harriet, "you've always liked chocolate. It's your favorite!" She looked at her son with a mixture of dismay and pleading.

"That's Evan. And Jo-jo. They like chocolate. I like angel food. That's my favorite." Billy did not look at his mother.

"*I* like chocolate," said Evan loyally.

"You can have my piece," said Billy, handing it across the table.

"Oh, but this is your going-away cake." Harriet had put her hand over her breast.

Billy shrugged.

"I've seen you eat chocolate, son," said Bill reproachfully.

"I don't like it very much. Anyway, it's not my favorite." He looked at his mother. "I've *told* you that."

"This is very inconsiderate, Billy," said his father. "Very inconsiderate of your mother."

"I'm sorry, honey," said Harriet.

"Nothing for you to be sorry about, mother," said Bill. He looked at his eldest son sternly.

Billy got up. "I'm going out for a while," he said.

Harriet asked, "But have you had enough to eat?"

"Yeah."

Bill glared at his son and rose abruptly as he crushed his paper napkin into a wad beside his plate. "Just a minute, son. I think you owe your mother an apology."

"What for?" Billy was sullen and refused to meet his father's eye.

"Oh, that's okay," said Harriet.

"You know damn well what for. We try to give you kids the best of everything, and then you behave like little snots. I'd sure like to know what's happened to gratitude."

"I just don't like chocolate," Billy mumbled.

"That's beside the point."

Billy stood uncertainly at the door.

"That's okay," Harriet repeated.

"You owe your mother an apology."

Billy looked at his feet and said, "I'm sorry."

"Don't worry about it, honey," said Harriet with self-conscious sadness.

"That's better," Bill huffed and resumed his seat.

Billy left the room as Evan asked, "Can I have another piece, mama? *I* like it."

Billy took his tan windbreaker off the hook on the hall closet door and carried it to the car. He started and raced the motor, then slammed the car into reverse and scattered gravel as he screeched out of the driveway. He wrenched into first gear, and the motor roared and tires squealed as he shot toward the stop sign at the end of the street where he stomped on the brake pedal so hard he lurched forward in spite of the grip he had on the door between his arm and ribs.

A car turned in front of him, and in the beam of his lights he saw Jo-jo sitting by the back-seat window, talking animatedly, a cigarette—more likely a joint—between his first finger and thumb. As Billy watched

in his rear view mirror, the car stopped in front of
their house, pausing at the curb instead of pulling
into the driveway, as though they were dropping off
a shipment of contraband, and had to make a quick
getaway. Jo-jo, jaunty and still laughing, got out. He
waved as the car sped off, the joint still between his
finger and thumb, its red glow creating an arc in
the darkness, and then he turned and swaggered
toward the house. Billy watched until he had disappeared behind the Russian olive, and still he waited,
as though he would be able to sense the impact of
Jo-jo's nonchalant entry on his father, mother, and
Evan. He was tempted to return, but instead he
turned left and entered the convoy of cars heading
west.

In Perryville he passed by the turnoff that led to
the Sheffields. His face grew warm and flushed as
he thought of Betty's softness, her perfume and
eagerness; he was frightened of what she seemed to
offer, and he could not steer the car toward her.

For an instant, like a flare on a battlefield, escape
into New York City illuminated his future. But the
city was, as Wilma said, scary.

He tried to recapture the early exhilaration of
being in his own car, cruising the cement network
of New Jersey, but riding with him, like an unwanted
passenger, was the realization that by this time tomorrow he would be back in the barracks. "Thought
your mother was dying of cancer," he could hear
them say; "Here comes the turkey." The golden

image of Jackson seared his inner eye. He pressed the accelerator and darted past and among the more sedately moving sedans and station wagons, goading drivers to blare their disapproval. Fuck 'em, he thought, rushing forward as though he had someplace to go.

For no reason he veered left off Kiowa Road onto a narrow, bumpy lane of cracked asphalt. The cars thinned after a few miles, as did the buildings. The seamy boundary of a town announced itself with a ring of burger joints and service stations that were dominated by a pink neon sign blinking "Barrel of Fun Bar" over a flat one-story building covered with red cedar shingles. Three cars were parked in front, and on impulse Billy pulled in beside them. Carrying his jacket jauntily over his shoulder, he left the car and sauntered into the building.

The smell—stale beer and smoke—and dim dankness brought back the memory of the sneaked evenings with Jackson over the pool table. There was no pool table here, but a bar on one side, and a rank of booths on the other. In front of the bar was a row of red plastic-topped round stools on chrome legs. Sitting near the door two men hunkered over their drinks, talking in low voices, and at the far end, a soldier wearing his garrison cap sat alone. Behind the bar a woman with a phone pressed onto her ear, held in place with one hunched shoulder, was drying glasses. She looked up vacantly and nodded without changing her expression as Billy entered.

He took a stool nearer the soldier than the two men, and the woman, followed by the longest phone cord he had ever seen, walked over to him. She raised her eyebrows questioningly, her attention focussed on what was flowing into her ear.

"A Bud," he said in a self-consciously deep voice.

One of the pair of men put money into the jukebox and a country-western wail filled the room, Tammy Wynette singing "Stand by Your Man." The barmaid brought a can of beer back and popped it open, then pointed back to the glasses on a shelf as she raised her eyebrows again. He shook his head no and took a swig from the can.

As his eyes grew accustomed to the darkness he assessed his neighbors. The two men looked suburban types in weekend mufti, still engrossed in their conversation, probably about home repairs. The soldier, he could see now, was a light-skinned black who sat ramrod straight in a uniform so creaseless it appeared to have been sprayed with acrylic, and he stared straight ahead at the mirror behind the bar. The barmaid was younger than Billy had thought. She moved languidly, still attached to the phone, like a cat on a leash.

"That girl been on that phone for half an hour," said the soldier quietly, tentatively, watching Billy in the mirror. "I wonder who she talking to." He laughed quickly.

"I don't know," said Billy, meeting his eye in the mirror. "Boyfriend, I guess." He too smiled.

The soldier softened and swiveled on his stool. "You from around here?" he asked.

Billy stiffened; he did not know any blacks, and he was uneasy at the instant affability, suspicious of ulterior motives. "No," he said shortly. "From another town."

"Me neither," said the soldier. "Shit. You couldn't *give* me this dump." He shook his head. "Man, *this* is what they call good times." His look swept the bar in disgust.

"Where you from?" Billy asked.

"South," said the soldier. "But I was in 'Nam for two years, and man, you can say what you want, but those Japs know how to live."

"In Vietnam?"

"Yeah. I was stationed there, but I went to Tokyo, Kyoto, you name it. I probably gonna settle there. Maybe. I'm in D.C. now," he added gloomily.

"What you doing here?"

The soldier's face switched to conventional sadness. In a hushed voice he said, "My daddy died. Home for the funeral."

"Oh, that's too bad, man," said Billy.

The soldier nodded. He held out his hand. "Name's Henry. Henry Long."

Billy introduced himself and they shook hands.

"Lemme buy you a drink," Henry said, casting off his mourning. He signaled the woman before Billy could answer. "So, what you doing here, Billy?" he asked after the beer had been placed in front of them by the woman, still listening intently to the phone.

"Oh, just . . . you know . . . home from school," Billy answered. "Just visiting my folks."

"Visiting your folks," Henry repeated, shaking his head. "Man, you're lucky you still got 'em." He sipped his beer, prolonging a pause. "I lost most of mine. Just got a few cousins and a sister." He shook his head. "Now that my daddy's dead, I don't have much left. You are one lucky man, you still got your folks."

"Yeah," said Billy, falling into his mood. "I sure am."

Henry looked down at the bar, and shook his head again. "I remember my daddy . . . that man would *die* for us kids. He would lay down in front of a *tractor* for us kids."

"Yeah, mine too," said Billy.

"Now my mother, she was *strict*. She was the lawgiver. Man, she wouldn't take no shit from *nobody*." He turned to Billy with a warning hand raised. "Now, don't get me wrong. That woman loved us kids, but she had, you know, *principles*."

"Yeah."

"But my daddy, he'd stand up for us kids. He'd say, 'Now Maureen, don't be so rough on those kids. They didn't mean nothing.' He'd say that when she was getting ready to stomp the shit out of us for something we'd done. You know, like she wanted us to amount to something."

"Yeah, man," Billy said.

Henry eyed the woman behind the bar. "I wonder what that guy's telling her," he said.

"What happened to your father?" Billy asked.

Moroseness dropped over Henry's features. "Cancer. Big C. Got my momma and daddy. Momma went about three years ago, and now daddy."

My mother's dying of cancer. "Gee, that's really bad," said Billy. He blushed in the dark.

"Yeah," Henry agreed, "it is." He stared thoughtfully at himself in the mirror behind the bar. "And Daddy was not a *old* man. Fifty-five. That ain't nothing today." Billy realized he was not sure how old his own father was. He puzzled about this for a few seconds while Henry stared silently at himself.

"He had a hard time," Henry continued gloomily. "Never held onto a job. That's why he was up here. One of his cousins thought he might be able to find something in Newark."

"My dad's had the same job for as long as I can remember," said Billy.

"That so?"

"Yeah. He's never let one of us kids do without anything we really needed. We're not, you know, rich or anything, but he's always provided for us."

"That a fact?" Henry was staring at the woman behind the bar intently.

"He's always made us, you know, work—I mean, we had to paint the house, and mow the lawn, and things like that—but he always got us what we needed.

All of us." Billy thought of Jo-jo's ingratitude with a small pop of anger. "Mother, too. She's always been there. She never did, you know, get one of those jobs. She stayed at home. She used to be a model."

"Yeah. Well, like I say, you're lucky you still got them." Henry smiled at the woman behind the bar who did not appear to notice him.

"You want another beer?" Billy asked. He felt at ease, in charge.

"Well, yeah, don't mind if I do. Thank you."

Billy raised his hand and signalled the woman who was leaning against the back counter. She looked at him questioningly and said something into the phone.

"Two Lites," he said authoritatively, having noticed what Henry was drinking. He was surprised at the loudness of his voice.

She nodded and got them, popped off the tabs and placed one in front of each.

"Thank you, ma'am," said Henry, looking at her intently, and brushing her hand with his.

She nodded and moved back to the rear wall, where she leaned against the counter as she fished out another glass to dry.

"Man," said Henry, "Whatever it is on the other end of that phone, it sure got her *hooked*."

"My dad is sending us all to college. I'm the first— I've got two brothers—and he's gonna put us all through school." Sudden gratitude, like a net dropped from the ceiling, entangled Billy, strangling not only his misery but also the memory of it. Expansively, he continued, "And, you know, even though he and Mom don't have much money, they gave me a car last year for my birthday."

"Ain't that something," said Henry noncommitally. "Sound like real nice folks. You got your own car, huh?"

"Yeah."

"Me, I gotta use my cousin's while I'm here. 'Don't you take that car into the City,' she said." Henry's voice slid into strident falsetto. "Man, if I had my own car I sure wouldn't be sitting in this shit-hole."

The bar was filling. On Billy's right a man and woman stopped their conversation and he felt their hostility, like the chill from an air-conditioned shop on a hot street.

"Yeah, well, it's not so bad," he said, lowering his voice.

"That's what you think," said Henry glumly. His eyes darted around the bar, registering disgust. "Hey, man," he said, as though with sudden inspiration, "what say you and me head for the city?"

"You mean, now?" asked Billy.

"Naw. I mean next Easter. Sure, man, I mean now. You got something holding you here?"

Escape into the city with this improbable companion entwined Billy like a tentacle. Henry would know the ropes. But there were too many unknowns. "Naw, man," he mumbled. "I got things to do here."

Henry shrugged. "Hmm. Yeah, man, well, you gotta do what you gotta do. Me I gotta get this car back to that old bitch before she calls out the state troopers."

"You gonna be around here for long?" Billy asked placatingly.

"Naw. Taking off tomorrow. Back to Washington. It's gonna look mighty good after this." He was disgruntled and bored. He got off the stool and glanced at the woman behind the bar. "Sure would like to know what she got on the other end of that line," he said. He held out his hand. "Be good, man."

Billy shook the hand, feeling suddenly forlorn. "I'm sorry about your dad."

"Yeah, well, that's the way it goes." Henry squeezed Billy's hand. "You enjoy yourself at that school down there—where is it?"

Billy told him.

"Never been there," said Henry, "but that don't mean nothing. I got out of the South quick-like." He was eager to be gone; his eye roved the bar restlessly. "So, see you around."

"Yeah. See you around."

Billy ordered another beer. The two men who had been talking at the end had been replaced by a man and woman; the latter was in a tight tee shirt and angry about something. The couple next to Billy exuded rays of distrust; one or the other would glance at him as though to make certain he was behaving himself. There was a booth of four men behind him who were loudly arguing in a superficially good-natured way. The woman behind the bar had finally hung up the phone but her expression had not changed; she seemed absorbed in a conversation no one else could hear, and gave the impression she would not notice if someone threw a stool through the mirror behind her.

Voices were raised sharply above the jukebox, which played a glut of country and western laments at maximum volume. The glow of companionable sentimentality that Henry had ignited dimmed in Billy. He felt it was just a matter of time before one or several of the patrons would turn on him, an outsider, and he decided to ease out before it happened.

A sharp chill had developed. Billy put his jacket on. He started the motor and gunned it twice reflectively, wondering where he would go. It was midnight, already Sunday morning.

A car pulled in beside him and he glanced over at it; there were four boys his own age, maybe a little older or younger, staring back at him. The familiar cold hollow opened in his belly, but he refused to drop his gaze and he and the occupants of the other car exchanged a silent, sullen challenge. Billy gunned his motor, growling his disdain, and the others fixedly watched him through the two layers of glass, silently menacing. To signal he was not fleeing, he sneered before looking over his shoulder in preparation to backing out. The boys in the other car laughed—he could see their derisive hostility aimed like a cannon across his bow. A chubby blond boy with full pink lips in the back seat lifted his fist, the third finger erect, priapic and scornful. Billy zoomed backwards, making the gravel fly, yanked the steering wheel to the right, and shot out of the parking lot onto the narrow road.

He sped down the bumpy, narrow road, his teeth gritted; carefully he stopped at a red light hanging over an intersection at which his was the only car. *Looks like we're gonna have to teach this Yankee faggot how to talk.*

The light changed to green, but he stayed, wavering, wondering which way to turn. A car pulled behind him and honked insistently. Billy lifted his fist, middle finger upright, so that it could be seen through his rear window, then jammed the accelerator and shot across the intersection.

He sped through a residential section, lined with bushes and trees and porchlights flickering through thinned autumnal leaves, back to Kiowa Road.

He turned toward Beaudale, gliding past an A&P and an Esso station, a McDonald's and a real estate office, each glowing emptily, spilling light onto vacant sweeps of parking lots where rows of slots were painted white on the murky asphalt. Cars rolled toward and behind him, moving at a civilized, orderly pace, each knowing its place, headlights courteously dimmed.

At Bradford Street he gave a left signal and turned off. He eased into the driveway quietly, out of consideration for family and neighbors; it was near one o'clock, and they would be sleeping. He was careful not to slam the car door, but pushed the catch into place by leaning against it.

The house was so quiet he could hear the hum of the refrigerator. He crept up the stairs past his parents' room—the sound of their steady breathing escaped through the half-open door—and into his own room. He switched on the light.

In the stark glare of the overhead bulb his room sprang harshly into relief; this was not the way he had remembered it at school, the brown bedspread so worn and faded in patches, the desk scarred, and the rug threadbare down the center. At the foot of the bed his mother had spread his suitcase, as though to remind him he was leaving; it lay yawning, with jeans, jockey shorts, shirts and rolled socks tucked into one side. His dress uniform still hung in the closet; he remembered he was supposed to wear it to church.

His shoulders sagged under the weight of his departure. Sitting on the edge of the bed, he looked at his feet as though he had never seen them before, studying the sneakers he had worn his last year of high school, with their frayed laces and puckered tongues.

Maybe the plane would crash, he thought. But, as his father said, air travel was safer than cars.

He opened his door softly and light from the room diffused into the hallway; the silence was accented by vague unidentifiable whispers and creaks, as though the house were breathing with his parents.

He walked soundlessly to their half-opened door and listened. Then he entered and went straight to the highboy near the closet. He glanced at the double bed and the two motionless forms in it. His father was on his back, pajamaed arms outside the blanket, and tucked near him, only her head above the covers, was his mother. He opened the top drawer of the dresser with a slight squeak and waited, watching the bed. His mother stirred, but did not waken. He reached into the drawer, his hand finding the leather pouch and feeling his way to the scored butt of the pistol. He pulled it out and cautiously closed the drawer. With the gun hanging at his side, he returned to his room and sat on the bed.

As he knew they would be, the chambers of the cylinder were loaded. His father had cleaned the gun after they returned from the range, and Billy could smell and feel the residue of oil that still clung to the dully gleaming barrel where "Smith & Wesson" had been stamped; with his index finger he traced the trademark, back and forth, thoughtfully, as the gun lay on his lap.

He lifted the barrel to his open mouth and rested it on his lower teeth, keeping his lips from touching it, as though he were saying "Ah" for a doctor. He brushed the trigger, then brought the slightest pressure to it; his arm tensed and his upper body grew cold with suspense. He had not released the safety catch.

He put the gun back in his lap. After a moment he lifted the gun to his temple, the barrel barely touching his hair above his ear, and pressed the trigger—gently, tenderly. He might faint and the gun would go off, or there might be a loud noise that would make him jerk the trigger. But the safety was still on.

He took the gun from his head, and released the safety catch. He put the barrel to his stomach, pressing it above his navel, then raised it beside his left nipple. His finger remained loosely on the trigger. He was breathing shallowly, his lips parted.

He lay the gun on the bed beside him and held his hands before him; they were steady, though he felt they should be trembling. He had almost stopped breathing.

He stood and clasped the gun around the butt, his finger on the trigger, and opened his door quietly. The even breathing of his parents dominated the stillness. He went to their door, as silent as the shadow he cast on the wall. Standing at the threshold, tense and alert, he waited until his eyes adjusted so he could see the outlines under the spread.

They had not moved. He took his gunfighter stance—sideways to the target, one arm outstretched—and aimed at the lump of his father. His finger tightened on the trigger, until he thought he could feel it give. His chest was icy, as though he were afraid, yet he was not. He held the pressure only for a second before lowering the gun and being rewarded with another rush of relief, like a celebration.

He returned to his room and shut the door, moving stealthily, and lowered himself to the bed so gently there was no creak of springs. He put one hand on the open suitcase spread at the foot of the bed; his right hand lay on his lap, the gun cradled in it. The black metal was warm, and its weight and solidity were comforting. He hefted the gun thoughtfully, then rose and went to the open closet where the dress uniform hung, immaculate. He closed the closet door and opened the door to the hall. Walking matter of factly and noiselessly, he entered his parents' bedroom.

He noticed staleness, the odor of confined air and used breath. Standing just inside the door he aimed at his father again, only this time he held the gun as he had been taught: both legs apart, both arms extended straight from his body at right angles, both hands steadying the gun as the muscles in his trigger finger tightened. He sighted the pale patch of forehead just below the thatch of hair that in the dim light appeared solid black. Gently he pressed the trigger. The explosion deafened him, but his arms did not recoil.

Harriet sat up, clutching the blanket to her throat. "What . . ." she said, blinded by sleep and terror, before the second explosion caught her in the chest and threw her back against the headboard.

His ears still ringing, he stepped into the hall. Jo-jo was standing outside the door where he and Evan slept, long spindly legs separated from his narrow chest by a pair of jockey shorts with a sagging waistband. When he saw Billy he laughed. "You crazy bastard," he said gleefully. "What are you doing?"

As Billy aimed at him, Jo-jo, grinning nervously, said, "Cut it out, you asshole. . . ." The shot caught him in the chest and knocked him against the doorframe. He fell with his feet in the hall and his torso on the rug in front of his bed.

Billy reached over him to the light switch inside the room. Evan was sitting up in bed staring at him, his mouth open. The shot caught him in the throat, and he half fell out of his bed, pulling the blanket, sheet, and bedspread with him.

Billy switched off the light and went back to his room. The smell of cordite pervaded the hall. He sat on his bed and looked at his hands. The barrel of the gun was hot against his thigh. Even though his ears were still ringing from the shots, he could hear the profound silence of the house.

Holding his breath, he sensed a sound that should not have been there, like a whisper, or a careful footfall. Cautiously he rose and went to his door, suddenly afraid.

He stood still, hoping the sound was his imagination, but he heard it again. It came from the doorway where Jo-jo's long naked legs protruded. Still carrying the gun, Billy tiptoed to the body and peered over it into the room. He could see nothing, but he heard a scuff, or maybe a sigh. He flipped on the light.

Evan was on the floor at the foot of his bed, crawling on all fours through a trail of his own blood, his head down. He stopped when the light came on but did not look up.

Billy's heart was wrung. He remembered a chipmunk he had once caught in a trap, crippling without killing it.

"Evan," he said, stepping over Jo-jo and coming into the room. "Go back to bed, Evan." He lifted the boy, surprised at his lightness. Evan was crying silently, with tiny gasps that made the blood spurt from his throat. He turned large terrified eyes on Billy, but did not resist. Billy laid him on the bed on his back and put his hand over his eyes and said, "It's just a bad dream, Evan. You're having a nightmare. Go back to sleep." He held the gun to his brother's ear and pulled the trigger, and felt the spasm of the body under his hand.

He turned off the light again and went back to his room, and this time the silence was undisturbed.

His window was black with night. He sat on his bed in the bright glare of the overhead light and began to feel a chill. Evan's blood on his tee shirt grew stiff to the touch.

He sighed and closed the suitcase at the foot of his bed and put it on the floor. Then he went down the hall to where Jo-jo lay on his back and switched on the light again. Blood had run from the wound in his narrow chest down on the rug, and there was a lot of it. Billy studied his brother for a moment, then went to their connecting bathroom and got a towel. He brought it to the body and wrapped it around the chest and then caught the body beneath the armpits and dragged it down the stairs and through the kitchen out into the yard and around to the garage. He eased the garage door up on its old hinges and pulled Jo-jo inside. He closed the door as quietly as possible, but in the still night the racket was magnified. He turned on the garage light and found, under a pile of cardboard boxes where his father stored old papers, a trunk that his grandmother had left when she went to California. He pried the lid open—the catch was stiff with disuse—and pulled out books, papers, souvenirs, a few musty clothes—stuff his mother had never gotten around to throwing out. He dragged Jo-jo's body—still limp, though cold—and folded the gangly bare legs so that he would fit into the womb of junk, then piled as many things as he could on top of it and still close the lid.

He paused, sweating, before taking off his stained tee shirt and stuffing it beside Jo-jo. Parts of Jo-jo—his hair, a foot, a hand—were visible, but he shut the lid of the trunk and shoved it back where it had been, and piled his father's boxes of papers back on top of it. He was cold in the night air without his tee shirt and walked quickly back to the kitchen and up the stairs.

He went into his parents' room, but did not turn on the light. His shot had taken the top off his father's head; beside Bill his mother half reclined, head lolling on her shoulder, her neck limp. The pillow beneath his father's head was soaked with blood, and he kept that in place as he grasped his father under the armpits and pulled him out of the bed. Bill's feet made a thump on the rug as they hit the floor. Keeping the pillow between his stomach and his father's mutilated head, Billy dragged him into Jo-jo's room, and put him sprawling half on, half off Jo-jo's bed. Billy checked his own naked torso for signs of blood, but found none. He carried Jo-jo's pillow back to his parents' bed and put it where his father's head had lain.

Back in his own room he discovered blood on his jeans. He took them off and laid them on the bed next to the gun.

He took a shower, letting the water run until steam rose from the tub and covered the mirror over the sink with mist; he stood in it until he felt warm. He dried himself, polished his glasses, and put on clean underwear, jeans, and tee shirt that he took from the suitcase.

He checked his room again, then gathered up the spotted jeans and the gun and his windbreaker before turning off the light and going down the stairs. Passing through the kitchen he went out into the yard and around to the garage.

In the garage he removed the papers and opened the trunk to drop in the gun and stuff the jeans beside it. Fastidiously, he avoided touching the parts of Jo-jo that were exposed. He slammed the lid, replaced the cardboard boxes, and brushed his hands to rid them of dust. Then he left the garage and closed the door.

He got into the Cobra, started the motor, and quietly backed out of the driveway onto Bradford Street. At the stop sign he carefully looked both ways before pulling on to Kiowa Road, which was deserted. He drove slowly toward the center of Beaudale, and just before he reached the old railroad crossing he saw a police car parked in the Friendly Foods lot, its interior light as well as its headlights on. Inside were two fat policemen drinking coffee from styrofoam cups. The driver, his huge face impassive, studied Billy a few seconds before lowering his window; the other policeman, as big as his partner, watched him out of flat emotionless eyes. The driver nodded, waiting for him to speak.

"Officer," Billy said, "My family's been shot. I think they're dead. My brother's gone. . . ."

Suddenly the enormity of what he had said clutched him in the gut and he sobbed. "I think they're all dead," he repeated.

Both policemen looked at him with open mouths.

"Where do you live?" asked the driver.

"2680 Bradford Street. I'm Billy Johnson. . . ."
He watched the policemen helplessly, waiting for
them to tell him what to do.

"Can you drive there? We'll follow you," said the
policeman.

Billy got into his car and pulled out onto Kiowa
Road, the police car behind him. He turned into his
driveway and shut off the motor and lights as the
police car stopped behind him. The two policemen
got out and came toward him and Billy led them to
the front door.

"Where are they, son?" asked the driver's partner.

"Upstairs. They're . . . . They were in bed."

The policemen had their guns out as they stalked
the house. "There's no one there," said Billy. "Just
. . . my folks."

As if they had not heard, the two men crept up
on the front door and the driver slammed it open
while they both pointed their guns at the dark interior. Cautiously, they entered. Billy started to follow, but the driver turned to him and said tersely.

"You wait out here, son."

They were gone about five minutes. When they
came back they were grave and subdued. "I guess
you better come in," said the driver gently, while
his partner went to the car. "Can you tell us when
you got home?" He put his huge hand solicitously
on Billy's shoulder, and led him into the house. "Just
take your time, son," he added gently.

Chapter Ten

BILLY SAT DAZED on the sofa as men came and went. Within minutes, it seemed, the house was full of people—solemn, questioning, respectful, curious, considerate. He had been asked if there was anyone he wanted to notify and he had called Gene.

"Oh, my God, my God," said Gene, "oh you poor kid. We'll be right there. Are you sure . . . ?" He had hung up, his question unfinished, and within half an hour he and Helen arrived, both white and stricken. Helen's little face beneath its huge bubble of solid golden hair was wizened, and lipstick was smudged off her thin lips.

"Jesus," said Gene as he entered the room. "I knew that fuckin' kid . . . ." He stopped when he saw Billy and tears poured down his cheeks. "Oh, goddam it, you poor kid." Billy cried with him, as Helen stood by and shook her head slowly.

The windows grew grey; odors of cigarette smoke and brewed coffee wafted into the living room. Billy stayed on the couch as a series of men with deferential, soft, sympathetic voices asked him questions: What time had he left? When had he gotten home? Had he touched anything? Had there been any trouble with his brother?

Billy answered carefully. Gene sat beside him, occasionally patting his knee awkwardly and shaking his head. When the detective asked about Jo-jo, Gene clenched his teeth for an instant, then interrupted, "That little bastard . . ." but broke off, and shook his head again.

The bodies were removed, each on a covered stretcher carried by two attendants, one black, one white. The black man gaped into the living room at Billy.

Billy watched the stretchers numbly, untouched by what had been so thoughtfully hidden from his view. The tall, long-faced man who appeared to be the detective in charge lowered his voice and asked, "Are you okay, son?"

"Yes, sir," Billy replied.

Gene squeezed his knee. Helen came into the living room, a wad of damp Kleenex in her hand, and asked, hopelessly, "Does anyone want any more coffee?"

Then, when it was still early in the morning, and the light coming through the window was not yet strong enough to cancel the lamp, everyone changed.

The men looked at him speculatively, with less sympathy, more curiosity. Conversations broke off when he passed on the way to the bathroom; when he came back to the living room Gene watched him out of eyes grown opaque with distrust. The tall, long-faced man asked if Billy had anything else he wanted to tell them.

No, he replied, he could think of nothing else.

Without actually moving, Gene distanced himself. He stopped squeezing Billy's knee.

The tall detective, still speaking quietly, but watching Billy with shrewdly squinted eyes, said, "We've found Jo-jo, Billy."

"Where was he?"

"In the garage. In a trunk. With the gun we think was the murder weapon."

Beside Billy, Gene was still.

"How'd he get there?" Billy asked.

"We thought maybe you might have some ideas about that," said the detective, not unkindly.

"No, sir."

The detective nodded, still watching him. "In the trunk there was a tee shirt and a pair of jeans. They have blood on them. We think they might be yours. We think the blood is probably that of one of the victims."

Billy said nothing.

"We've sent the gun to be checked for fingerprints and the clothes to be tested."

Billy nodded.

"Maybe you'd be willing to take a lie detector test," the detective asked gently.

"Why?"

"Just to clear things up."

Gene watched Billy as alertly as one of his Doberman pinschers. Helen brought a tray of cups with a fresh pot of coffee and put it on the table in front of them; she had reapplied her makeup, her lips neatly outlined in red, her eyes rimmed in mascara, the lids a light blue. She left quickly without looking at Billy.

Billy shrugged. "Sure," he said.

"We'll have to go to Hackensack—that's the nearest polygraph equipment. You ready to go now?"

"Sure."

"Just a minute," said Gene belligerently, "what about a lawyer?"

The detective looked at him blandly. "Billy's not a suspect. He's not under arrest. This is just routine."

Gene wavered between skepticism and outrage. He appeared to be searching for the right reaction.

"In fact," the detective continued, "we're going to take Billy by headquarters and fingerprint him. Just routine."

Gene looked at his hands. "If that's the way you do it," he said unhappily.

"We'll read Billy his rights, if it comes to that," said the detective amiably.

"Whatever you say," Billy agreed.

He picked up his tan windbreaker and stood. Gene stood also, awkward and confused.

"We'll wait here for you," he said, but did not touch him.

Billy left by the front door with the detective. Little metal rods had been implanted around the yard and across the front, and strung through them was a thin rope on which cardboard "Scene of Crime" signs had been hung. As Billy got into the police car he saw a small group of people standing at the corner, in front of the Hardins' house, watching him. He recognized none of them.

"What're they doing here?" he asked.

The detective raised his eyebrows and shrugged.

At the police station Billy's fingers and thumbs were inked and imprinted and he was left alone in a concrete room with four metal chairs and a large wooden table. The windows were high and had mesh over them. He was cold.

The detective came in with another man and said, "We have something we want to read to you, Billy. Pay attention. Make sure you understand what I'm saying." Then he quickly read his rights in a monotonous rapid voice. "Okay? Any questions?"

"No, sir."

"Now then, we'd like for you to give us a formal statement. Just routine. Mr. DeGreco here will take it down."

Billy told them again how he had come home and found his family dead and his brother missing. He answered pretty much the same questions he had answered before. He was forthright and calm.

Mr. DeGreco glanced at him from time to time; the detective watched him steadily. When he was finished he gazed back at both of them.

After a pause, the detective said, "I guess we better go get that polygraph test. That'll clear everything up." He watched Billy a few seconds before adding, quietly, "You know, no one can fool those lie detectors."

"Yes, sir," said Billy. He knew people could fool the machines. It was just a matter of keeping calm.

The detective and an officer accompanied him in the police car to Hackensack. At the headquarters there he was led to a small room where a table of equipment had been placed behind a large chair which had wide wooden armrests.

"Here's the release," the detective said pleasantly, handing him a piece of paper.

"What's this?"

"Just a release, saying you give us permission to administer the polygraph test. You want to clear this up as quick as you can, don't you?"

"Sure." Billy signed the paper and handed it back without reading it.

Wires were attached to his arms by another man— older, patient-looking, and untidy—who then started asking him questions like, What am I holding in my hand? as he showed Billy a pencil, and leading to,

Would you ever harm anyone you loved? and Did you kill your family?

Billy answered them all calmly.

After he was finished he asked the detective, "How did I do?"

"How do you think you did?" the detective shot back, watching him.

"Okay, I guess."

The detective watched him closely. "We think you did it, Billy," he said.

Billy said nothing.

"You flunked the test. The test shows you lied."

Billy looked at the graph paper the detective was holding in front of him. "Did you do it, Billy?"

Billy was silent.

"Let's go back to Beaudale, Billy. I think you'd better give us another statement."

Billy was very tired. On the ride back to the Beaudale police station he thought he would like to go to sleep, but he was too tense. He had been awake for over 24 hours. He thought he was probably hungry, but he was so numb he could not be sure.

The detective and the policeman and the driver all grunted monosyllables among themselves, nothing of interest to him. He was grateful to them for not bullying or yelling at him.

When they arrived at the police station Billy wanted to call Gene, but he said nothing. The detective and policeman led him into the same bare room where he had sat while waiting to be fingerprinted, only this time they stayed with him while Mr. DeGreco was summoned.

"I think Billy wants to tell us something," said the detective pleasantly when the court reporter arrived.

Mr. DeGreco sat with his fingers poised over his machine and looked expectantly at Billy, who remained silent. The room was so quiet Billy could hear his own breathing. The three men waited for him to speak. He did not feel threatened, however, because they were so patient and quiet.

"What about it, Billy? You ready now to tell us what happened?" the detective asked conversationally.

"I told you," said Billy.

The detective smiled ruefully, but said nothing, just looked at him kindly.

Billy laughed nervously. "I mean, what more do you want?"

Still smiling, the detective said, "Why don't you tell us why you put Jo-jo's body in the trunk?"

Billy knew he should have denied putting Jo-jo's body in the trunk, but it did not seem worth the effort. Instead, he silently regarded the detective's friendly eyes for a while before dropping his own. He sighed deeply and replied, almost mumbling, "I thought it would look like he had done it."

The detective nodded understandingly.

"You put your father's body in Jo-jo's room. Why was that?"

Billy looked at the high window through which the afternoon sunlight, brilliant and clean, was shining. "There was a lot of blood where Jo-jo had . . . uh . . . fallen, and I knew I'd have to explain that, so . . . ." He shrugged.

"You thought, then, that we would think Jo-jo had done it," said the detective quietly.

Billy did not answer.

The detective gently prodded him. "You have to speak up so the reporter can take down your statement, Billy."

Billy said, "Well, yeah. I guess."

"You guess that you wanted us to think that Jo-jo had done it?"

"Yeah. I suppose."

The three men watched him with no expression. They did not seem outraged or upset. Billy relaxed under their detached scrutiny.

"Do you want to tell us now exactly what happened?" the detective asked sympathetically, as though he were a guidance counselor trying to help him through a particularly difficult problem.

Billy looked at his hands. "Yeah, I guess so," he said. And he told them everything he had done that evening: about the meal, the chocolate cake, the talk with Henry, the return to the house. The words flowed from him; he was too tired to censor or even listen to them. He spoke slowly, and sometimes fatigue thickened his tongue and he mumbled, but he told them everything he could remember. His eyes were dry and scratchy from lack of sleep.

He was relieved when he finished, but the detective had questions, and then more questions. Other men came and left, some looked at him oddly, some with hostility, but no one spoke harshly to him. Someone brought a sandwich, and he wolfed it down, scarcely tasting it, and all the while the questions continued, going over and over the same ground, until he became confused and petulant.

"But I *told* you that," he said crossly several times.

"I know, Billy," the detective answered, placating and soothing. "We just want to get it straight. Now, the reason you did this was because you did not want to go back to school."

"I told them I couldn't go back." He took his glasses off to rub his eyes.

"So you killed your family to avoid returning to school?"

Billy did not like the question put that way. The silence following it was expectant; he felt defensive and did not answer.

Gently, the detective asked, "Is that why you killed your family, Billy . . . ? To keep from going back to school?"

Without his glasses, the men were outlines with blurred faces, and corners and windows lost their edges. He held the glasses limply on his lap. "I guess so," he said softly.

As though this was what they were waiting for, the men stirred; Billy could feel the change in the room. He was so weary it was hard for him to hold his mouth shut. Fluorescent lights, which had been on all the time, now furnished the only illumination, and shone hard and implacable above him. He put his glasses back on and the outlines of people and objects filled in. There were five men in the room, but they did not appear to be paying him much attention; they were talking among themselves, scribbling on forms, drinking coffee. Only the uniformed policeman at the door seemed to be watching him, but indifferently.

"I'm tired," he said.

Some of the men glanced at him, but only the detective responded. "We're almost finished, Billy."

In a little while—he had lost track of time—he was led to a cell to spend the night. He was so exhausted he did not even want to take off his clothes, but he did so at the urging of the detective, who said he would be more comfortable in his underwear. He crawled onto the hard cot and pulled the blankets around his throat. The light from the corridor—fluorescent and harsh like that in the room he had just left—shone into the cell through the bars, but when he closed his eyes and turned to the wall, he found darkness.

He did not know whether he was awake or asleep, but suddenly he was learning to swim. He was frightened, yet he could feel the support of his father's hand on his belly, keeping him afloat.

"Don't thrash," Bill shouted. "You'll drown if you thrash around like that."

He kicked and flailed at the water, and suddenly he sank, terrified because he could not breathe. Then he was raised to the surface again, and his father was saying, "See what happens when you get scared? Just take it easy." He kept kicking and moving his arms, and then he was swimming, gliding through the water, cutting it like a knife, skimming over it, and it seemed nothing could stop him.